S.P.E.A.R.

CHRIS BRADFORD

Illustrated by Neil Evans

onkers

First published in 2019 in Great Britain by
Barrington Stoke Ltd
18 Walker Street, Edinburgh, EH3 7LP

www.barringtonstoke.co.uk

Text © 2015, 2016, 2017, 2019 Chris Bradford
Illustrations © 2015, 2016, 2017 Neil Evans

The moral right of Chris Bradford and Neil Evans
to be identified as the author and illustrator of this work has
been asserted in accordance with the Copyright, Designs and
Patents Act, 1988

A CIP catalogue record for this book is available
from the British Library upon request

ISBN: 978-1-78112-849-7

Printed and bound by CPI Group (UK) Ltd, Croyden, CR0 4YY

Renfrewshire
Council

The library is always open at
renfrewshirelibraries.co.uk

Visit now for
homework help
and free
eBooks.

We are the Skoobs and we love the library!

Phone: 0300 300 1188
Email: libraries@renfrewshire.gov.uk

To Hayley, my Guardian Angel

Contents

PART 1: BULLETCATCHER

1. Gunfire 3

2. Army of Freedom 7

3. Medusa 12

4. Best Hope 18

5. S.P.E.A.R. 22

6. Reactor Room 31

7. Apollo 39

8. One Second Fighting 47

9. Mission Pandora 53

10. Tattoo 61

11. Hero Gene 69

12. Double Vision 75

13. Sacrifice 84

14. Bulletcatcher 92

PART 2: SNIPER

15. Glint of Sunlight 99

16. Bullet Ears 105

17. The Judge 112

18. Zanshin Zone 119

19. Funfair 124

20. Bait 133

21. Unbroken Shield 140

22. Blackout 143

23. Blood 150

24. Face I.D. 153

25. Subway 158

26. Shock to the System ... 163

27. The Verdict 169

28. Doubt 175

PART 3: BLOWBACK

29. Messenger 183

30. All Gone 187

31. Battle Booster 192

32. Fortress 199

33. Judgement Day 209

34. Code Red 215

35. Safe Room 223

36. The Trial 229

37. Execution 236

38. Back from the Dead 243

39. Line of Fire 250

40. Divine Justice 254

41. Hidden Talent 258

42. Free Choice 264

EXTRAS

Do YOU have what it takes
to be a bulletcatcher? 272

Do YOU have
superpowers? 276

Go Gear 279

Quick-fire interview
with *S.P.E.A.R.* author
Chris Bradford 280

PART 1

Bulletcatcher

1. GUNFIRE

The Near Future

Troy looked up from the Batman comic he was reading and locked eyes with a girl on the other side of the display stand.

The girl was geek-pretty with brown eyes, a silver nose stud and short black hair bleached white at the tips. She stopped bobbing her head to the silent beat from her headphones and smiled sweetly at Troy. Only then did he realise he was staring at her.

Troy attempted to smile back but his lips seemed to have frozen solid. He was always shy in front of girls, even girls reading retro comics on a

Saturday morning in Terminus City's grand mall.

Troy stuck his head back in his comic to hide the red flush rising in his cheeks. *Fourteen years old*, he thought, *and I've never had a girlfriend, or been kissed! It's just embarrassing, and depressing.*

Then he heard the sound of gunfire. For a moment Troy thought it was his imagination. Sometimes he got so lost in a comic that the story seemed more real than the world around him. But as he turned the page to see Batman punch out one of the Joker's henchmen, he heard it again. Gunshots, followed by screaming.

This time he knew he *wasn't* imagining it.

The store owner – a chubby man with a ponytail and half-moon glasses – peered out into the mall. A woman ran past, wide-eyed with terror.

Troy dumped the Batman comic and ran over to the window. "What's going on?" he asked.

The store owner shook his head. "No idea."

Both of them flinched as another round of gunfire echoed through the mall. They stared as men, women and children fled in every direction. A few shoppers stood frozen in shock, while others cowered behind pillars and hid behind litter bins.

More gunshots. The fast-food place opposite emptied in a flash. People knocked over tables and chairs in their rush to escape. Only one man remained. He lay across a table as spilt ketchup dripped onto the floor below.

It took a moment for Troy to realise it wasn't ketchup at all. It was blood.

Sickened at the sight, at last Troy grasped what was happening. The mall was under attack! He felt a surge of sheer panic – what to do next? His parents had gone for a coffee on the first floor. Should he go and find them? Should he stay where he was? Or should he run?

Troy pressed his face against the glass,

scanning for his parents among the fleeing crowd. But the mall was in total chaos. He was about to give up hope when he spotted them race down the escalator and towards the comic store.

"The A.F.!" he heard his father scream. "*Run, Troy, run!*"

2. ARMY OF FREEDOM

Troy knew from the TV news that A.F. stood for "Army of Freedom" – a terrorist group that launched random violent attacks on Terminus City and its people. He'd never been caught up in anything like this before. He'd always imagined that such horror and tragedy happened to other people. Not to him and his family.

Troy stared out the window of the comic store as five people in black combat trousers and black hooded jackets marched down the glossy walkways of the mall. Their faces were hidden behind blank white masks. Only their eyes could be seen through the two slits in the plastic. The lead terrorist strode along like some faceless terminator, firing his compact F4000 assault rifle at anything that moved.

Troy watched helpless as the terrorist swung the gun to point at his parents. "LOOK OUT!" he screamed.

But Troy's warning came too late.

The F4000 thundered in the man's grip. Bullets flew.

Troy's mother went down first.

His father stopped to pull her up. A bullet clipped his arm and spun him round. But he still managed to dive on top of her body to shield her.

The terrorist fired again.

His parents' bodies jerked in the storm of bullets, then lay still.

A cry of horror rose up in Troy's throat. He pounded at the window in despair. Then the terrorist turned to face him and opened fire. Troy threw himself to the floor as the store window shattered. Shards of glass rained down on him.

He heard screams as the other customers fled for the back exit. But Troy was frozen rigid with fear, too horrified by his parents' deaths to move.

The store owner slammed the front door shut and tried to lock it. In his panic he seemed to have forgotten that a glass door would be no match for an automatic rifle firing ten rounds per second. Bullets shattered the door and flung the store owner back. He landed in a bloody, broken heap by the sales desk.

The masked terrorist stepped inside.

Only now did some survival instinct impel Troy to move.

He scrambled to his feet, shoved away a comic stand and darted for the rear exit. The stand skidded across the floor and hit the terrorist. It knocked off his aim, and bullets ripped into a shelf of magazines instead of Troy.

Troy looked back and saw that the man's hood had come down. He caught a flash of shaved blond hair and a small black tattoo behind the man's left ear before the terrorist batted away the comic stand and took aim again.

But Troy wasn't the target any more. It was the cute girl who'd smiled at him earlier.

She was curled up in a ball on the floor. Troy could see that she was trembling with fear. He sprinted in her direction, flew forwards and landed on top of her. The terrorist's machine gun roared and Troy felt the first of the deadly bullets hit him.

3. MEDUSA

Troy woke to a strange electronic *beep ... beep ... beep ...*

His eyes flickered open and he saw that there were sensors attached to his bare chest. He lay in a hospital bed in a white room with no windows. A bank of hi-tech medical monitors displayed his heartbeat and other vital signs. The screens gave off a soft green glow.

As his eyes came into full focus, Troy saw a tall woman standing at the end of his bed. Her hair was a shock of twisted white spikes. This extreme style seemed at odds with the smart silver-grey business suit, leather gloves and long silver earrings that she wore. Her thin lips stretched in a friendly smile but the warmth didn't reach her eyes, which were as cold and grey as stone.

"How are you feeling, Troy?" she asked in a clipped English accent.

"All right ... I think," he replied as he sat up in the bed. His muscles felt stiff and sore and he could see a dark line of bruises on his left-hand side, but that seemed to be the worst of it.

"A miracle, after what happened to you." The woman held up an ultra-thin glass pad and pressed the "play" icon on the screen. "This is—"

"Who are you?" Troy interrupted. "Are you a doctor?"

"I'm Medusa," she said, and she thrust out a gloved hand as if she had only just remembered her manners. Then she pointed to the screen. "As I was saying, this is from a CCTV camera at the time of the terrorist attack."

Troy looked at the screen and saw a scrawny

white kid with cropped sandy hair and a gawky manner in the comic store. Himself – no wonder he had no luck with girls!

On the screen, the shop window shattered and Troy dropped to the floor.

"Fast reactions," Medusa remarked.

Now the terrorist entered and Troy pushed the magazine stand and ran for the exit.

"Good thinking to use the stand to throw off the gunman's aim," Medusa said with a curt nod of approval.

Troy hadn't meant to hit the terrorist at all. The stand had just been in his way. But he didn't correct her.

Next he saw himself dive on top of the girl.

"That was brave of you to try to save her," Medusa said.

"But I ... I didn't," Troy stammered.

Medusa smiled at him. "Don't be so modest," she

said. "The girl's alive and well, thanks to you."

On the screen the terrorist's gun went on blasting out bullets. Troy's heart raced at the sight of his body shuddering with each shot.

"Turn it off! Please!" he begged. He couldn't bear to watch any more of the brutal assault. It reminded him about what had happened to his parents.

Medusa swiped the screen and the image disappeared.

"I'm glad the girl's OK, but how did we ever survive *that*?" Troy asked.

"My dear," Medusa replied, "*you* survived because you're bulletproof."

Troy stared at her. "You are joking, aren't you?"

But this mysterious woman didn't look like the sort of person who made jokes.

"You saw it for yourself," Medusa said. "That terrorist shot you at point-blank range with over 15 high-velocity 45mm rounds. Not even a soldier's

Kevlar body armour vest could have stood up to an attack like that."

"But that's impossible," Troy said. He now believed he was either dead, dreaming or delusional. He pinched himself but he didn't wake up.

"No, it's not impossible," Medusa said. "You're not like most humans. The cells of your skin have an unusually high carbon content and are arranged in a honeycomb pattern. When you're hit by a bullet, your skin can harden and spread the energy over a large area. This means your body can withstand ten times the impact that steel can."

Troy's jaw dropped open in shock. He remembered how he'd been hit by a car the year before as he fled from a gang of bullies. The paramedic on the scene said he should have been killed. But Troy hadn't even broken a bone. At the time everyone thought he'd just been very lucky.

"Are you saying I'm like ... *Superman?*" he asked.

Medusa let out a snort of laughter. "No, dear, you don't have his strength or his looks, I'm afraid. But with the right training, we could make you into a super*boy*."

Troy frowned. "Training? What are you talking about?"

Medusa smiled her cold smile. "Troy," she said. "I'm here to recruit you as a bulletcatcher."

4. BEST HOPE

"I head up S.P.E.A.R., a secret protection agency,"
Medusa explained as Troy lay in his hospital bed and
listened with growing amazement. "S.P.E.A.R. provides
security for the rich and powerful in Terminus City. A
lot of the time we work with the sons and daughters
of important families. Our services are needed more
than ever with the increased threat from terrorists
like the A.F. That means we need more recruits—"

"You mean there are others like me?" Troy asked.

Medusa nodded. "Yes, but they all have different
talents."

Troy sank back on his pillow, stunned by what
he was hearing.

"You have the natural instinct and the physical

talent to be a bulletcatcher," Medusa stated. "All you have to do is sign this release form and we can begin your training."

She held out the pad again. A digital contract was on the screen. Troy looked at it and all of a sudden he realised what she was saying.

"I can't be a *bodyguard*!" he protested. He pushed the pad away. "You've got the wrong guy. I'm always the *last* one anyone chooses for sport at school. No one would want *me* as their bulletcatcher. I was scared to death in that mall. I just wanted to escape."

"That's the best response in a crisis," Medusa replied. "Escape – get yourself and the VIP out as fast as you can."

"I ... I can't be a bulletcatcher," Troy insisted. "I have to go back to school."

"And *who's* going to make sure you get to school?" Medusa asked.

"My mu—" Troy began. Then he felt his breath

cut off as he remembered again that his mother and father were dead. Murdered in cold blood by an A.F. terrorist. Troy choked back a sob and stared up at the ceiling as his eyes stung with tears.

"I am very sorry for your parents' deaths," Medusa said. She sat on the edge of Troy's bed and gave his arm a soft pat. "It must be hard for you. Our records show you have no other family in Terminus City. You're alone in this world. So, what are you going to do? You can't go back to Poland. You have no family left there either. Where are you going to live? How are you going to survive?"

Troy swallowed hard and tried to fight back the tears. He didn't have any answers.

"You're an orphan, Troy, and your parents were immigrants," Medusa went on. "In this city, children like you don't last long. And no one can adopt. Not with the Council's One Family, One Child policy. But S.P.E.A.R. will take care of you."

She put the digital release form in his hands.

"I ... don't know," Troy said. He felt utterly lost and desperate.

"Join S.P.E.A.R. It's your best hope," Medusa urged.

Troy looked at her. Her stone-grey eyes seemed to fill his blurred vision. She was right. *What other choice did he have?*

5. S.P.E.A.R.

"Welcome to S.P.E.A.R. HQ," Medusa said as her car came to a stop outside a run-down old building.

After Troy had signed the release form with his fingerprint, Medusa had taken him to his parents' tiny rented flat. They had collected his few belongings and arranged for the rest of his family's possessions to be put in storage. The only item that was of any value to Troy was a photo of him with his parents. He'd pocketed this before he left the flat to start his new and unexpected life as a bulletcatcher.

Troy peered out the car's tinted windows at the crumbling red-brick building.

"It's a library!" he said in astonishment.

"Exactly," Medusa said. "It's the perfect cover. Now everything is online, who goes to a library any more?"

"I do," Troy admitted. He felt like more of a geek than ever.

Medusa raised a thin eyebrow at him. "Why doesn't that surprise me? Now follow me."

The doors of the car opened and Medusa led Troy up the stone steps. Inside the place was deserted – there was only an outmoded library bot on duty.

The bot tracked their movements as Medusa headed over to the lift. They stepped inside and she pressed her thumb to an ID scanner. The lift juddered then went down. Troy watched the floor number drop from 0 to –1, to –2 ... and then it went blank. But still the lift went down.

Troy was about to ask if the lift was broken when the doors opened onto a gleaming silver and white reception area. Discreet lighting glowed ultraviolet blue, and glass displays on the walls showed news feeds and security updates from around the world. The reception was so sleek and hi-tech that Troy felt as if he'd stepped onto a starship.

A security guard stood to attention at the desk and greeted Medusa. Behind the guard Troy spied a CCTV monitor with a video image of the library they'd just walked through. The library bot must really be a surveillance droid!

"Where's Kasia?" Medusa demanded.

"On her way," the guard replied. "I've pinged her. *Several* times."

Medusa's lips thinned in irritation. Then a girl in a pink workout top and grey joggers strolled along the curved corridor towards them. She had platinum-blonde hair, snow-white skin and bewitching ice-blue eyes. She reminded Troy of his cousin Anna in Finland. He'd only ever seen Anna in a photo, but the two girls shared the same striking looks.

"Timing is everything, Kasia," Medusa said in a stern tone. "You should know that as a bulletcatcher."

"Time is all about how you see it," Kasia replied. Her attitude was as ice-cool as her looks.

Medusa narrowed her eyes in warning. "Kasia, show our new recruit around and introduce him to the others," she snapped. "And don't be late again!"

Medusa told Troy that she would see him later and then strode off down the corridor.

Her high heels clicked on the polished marble floor.

Kasia gave Medusa a salute. "Yes, your highness," she said under her breath. Then she turned to Troy. "Medusa is all right but she can be a real taskmaster at times," she said with a smirk. "So, you're Troy?"

Troy nodded.

"Is it true? Did you *really* stop a bullet?" she asked.

Troy gave another nod.

Kasia whistled. "Impressive! And do you speak at all?"

Troy nodded again. He was entranced by her blue eyes and he'd become totally tongue-tied.

Kasia laughed. "I look forward to it. Come with me. Let's get this tour over with, then we can chill."

She led him along the corridor to a door marked with an emerald green logo. It showed a graphic of a spearhead and the letters S.P.E.A.R. ran down its centre.

Troy finally plucked up the courage to speak. "What does S.P.E.A.R. stand for?"

"Security, Protection and Elemental Assault Response," Kasia replied.

"Elemental?" Troy said.

"It refers to the natural superpowers a bulletcatcher like you has," Kasia said, and she pressed her thumb to the ID scanner.

The door slid open and they entered a huge round chamber. They were on an upper gallery looking down onto a sunken floor. Three circles of padded seats sloped to the centre of the chamber where there was a large hologram desk. Above this hung four mega screens.

"This is our briefing room for missions," Kasia explained. She pointed to a row of doors on the far side of the chamber. "That's our accommodation block. Your bed cell is the one on the far right with the blue border."

She walked him round the upper gallery. "Here's our main classroom ... and this is the fitness gym and combat zone."

Troy peered through a narrow window and saw stacks loaded with heavy weights, a row of resistance machines, six treadmills and a martial arts dojo. "Why do you have a gym?" he asked. "I thought everyone used Fit Pills."

"If only!" Kasia laughed. "Our combat instructor is old-school. He believes you can't get truly fit without real sweat and tears. His motto is 'No blood, no guts, no glory.' So be prepared to *bleed* in your training. Literally!"

Troy's eyes widened in alarm. He wasn't a natural athlete and the Fit Pills had been far too expensive for his family to ever use.

Kasia gave him a kind smile. "Don't worry, it's not all bad. The food is good and we don't ever go without," she said. She showed him a large dining area filled with the mouth-watering aroma of *real* food. Troy had forgotten what it was like – like most of the population he had grown up on synthetic meals.

Kasia carried on with the tour. "We also have

a state-of-the-art Rec Room with GameChairs, a virtual cinema and even a Prism Table – but Lennox broke one of the laser cues last week."

"A Prism Table?" Troy exclaimed. "Are you serious?" He had only ever seen one on TV before.

"Well, if you like the sound of that ..." Kasia said as she stopped outside a door with a red border. "You're going to love the Reactor Room."

6. REACTOR ROOM

The door slid open and a small black ball rocketed towards Troy's head. Troy had no time to avoid it. But in the blink of an eye Kasia stepped forward and caught the missile in mid-air. Just millimetres from Troy's shocked face.

"Spoilsport!" a stocky kid with an American accent called. He sat at a control desk in a small darkened room. "We all know Troy can stop a bullet, but I wanted to see if he could *dodge* one."

"Meet Lennox, the joker of our pack," Kasia said. She tossed the ball back at the boy. Lennox ducked. But with the build of a trainee pro wrestler, he struggled to avoid the returning shot.

Kasia looked at Troy. "What are you staring at?"

Troy was still amazed at the speed of her reaction to the attack. "How did you move so fast?" he asked.

Kasia shrugged. "My talent is reflex. I react six times faster than most humans."

"6.8 times faster, to be exact," a skinny boy with short brown hair and glasses corrected her. He was sitting hunched over a computer and his fingers flew across the touchscreen even as he spoke. "Kasia's metabolic rate is double normal levels," he explained. "She also has enhanced visual powers. Her eyes react faster and absorb three times more data in one second than a normal human's eyes. Her brain processes this data faster too, so Kasia can make rapid decisions. So, when she's on full alert, she experiences time as if it's passing in slow motion. Basically, Kasia is like a fly."

"Thanks, Joe," Kasia said. Her voice dripped

with sarcasm. "You do know how to pay a girl a compliment!"

Joe looked up at her with a frown on his face. "It wasn't a compliment. It's a fact."

Kasia rolled her eyes at him and he went back to his manic typing.

"Why don't you show Troy what you can really do?" said a voice from the corner of the room. Troy spun round to see an Asian girl in a purple T-shirt and dark glasses, her long dark hair twisted into a high bun.

Kasia sighed. "I'm not a circus act, Azumi."

"Joe's spent the day upgrading the Reactor software," Lennox said in a teasing tone. "I bet you can't beat the system now."

Kasia rose to the challenge. "Fifty credits says I do."

"You're on!" Lennox agreed with a grin.

A side door opened and Kasia disappeared into

the main Reactor Room. Troy joined Lennox and Joe at the control desk. They peered through a window and saw Kasia standing in the middle of a circular room with a domed roof. The walls were glowing white, with thousands of faint circles dotting the surface.

The lights in the control room dimmed and the Reactor Room transformed into a street scene teeming with people and cars.

"This is a simulator," Joe explained. "It creates a real-world experience. The avatars have their own personalities and you can interact with them. We use this system to practise dealing with attacks on VIPs. With regular training sessions, the system can improve a bulletcatcher's response time to a threat by up to 50%. This could mean the difference between life and death on a real mission."

Kasia was observing the virtual crowd when a man appeared with a handgun. A hard black ball shot out from a circle in the wall, as if it had come from the weapon. Kasia had little trouble avoiding the speeding bullet.

"The scene and people may be virtual, but those balls are real," Lennox explained as Kasia sidestepped another attack. "You *don't* want to be hit by one."

"Think of this like an ultra-fast and painful form of dodgeball," Azumi said.

"Time to test the upgrade … and Kasia," Joe said. He slid a finger across the control panel.

All of a sudden, multiple attackers appeared. But Kasia evaded them all with ease. She bobbed and weaved and darted round the room at lightning speed.

"She's like Neo from *The Matrix*!" Troy said.

"The *what*?" Lennox asked with a frown.

"It's an old sci-fi movie," Troy said as Kasia ducked, dived and dodged the balls flying in all

directions across the Reactor Room.

After five minutes, the system ran out of ammo and the session ended. Kasia came back into the control room, out of breath but unhurt.

"You owe me fifty credits, Lennox," she said, and she held out her hand.

With a reluctant grunt, Lennox fished in his pocket for a transfer chip.

Kasia looked at Troy. "Fancy a go?"

Troy shook his head. "Looks far too hard for me."

"I'll re-set it to beginner mode," Joe said. "We can start when you're ready."

Troy realised he no longer had an excuse and so he stepped inside the Reactor Room. A few seconds later, a restaurant scene appeared. Guests sat at tables while others chatted by the bar.

Troy could hear a piano in the background and a waiter was moving among the guests with a tray of drinks. But Troy couldn't spot any obvious attackers. Then a pretty blonde girl in a short satin dress came up to him.

"Hi, handsome," she said with a dazzling smile.

As she waltzed past, Troy couldn't take his eyes off her.

"Excuse me, sir, would you like a drink?" the waiter asked.

Troy turned to the waiter to say no and found himself staring into the barrel of a gun. A black ball shot out and hit him dead centre in the forehead.

7. APOLLO

"Not the best place to catch a bullet!" Kasia smirked the next morning as she admired the perfect circle of a red mark on Troy's forehead.

The team were gathered in the fitness gym for their first training session of the day. Troy stared down at the floor. He was still embarrassed by his swift defeat in the Reactor Room.

"Don't worry," Lennox said. He slapped Troy on the back and almost snapped his spine. "I fell for Jinx too. Who wouldn't? She's hot."

"Jinx is a program sub-routine," Joe said. "She's designed to distract the user before an attack and to teach you how important it is to focus during a—"

"WHAT A BUNCH OF MISFITS, NERDS, WIMPS

AND SLOBS YOU LOT ARE!" A colossal man in a red tracksuit had appeared and was thundering at them.

Troy had been warned by Kasia at breakfast that their fitness and combat instructor was a fearsome man, but nothing could have prepared him for Apollo. He had a shaven head and was the size of a bull. He looked just as strong ... and just as mean.

"You know the drill!" Apollo bawled. "You get your warm-up done *before* I get here. Now go, go, GO!"

There was a groan from the team as they got onto the treadmills and began running. Troy stepped onto his machine and searched for the start button.

"Let's see what you've got, Troy," Apollo said. He stabbed the display to life and held down the speed button.

Troy's legs went from under him and he had to sprint just to stay on the machine. When he was happy that Troy was going fast enough, Apollo moved on to Lennox. He was walking.

"Come on, Fatty, shift!" Apollo said, and he pressed the speed button.

"I'm not fat," Lennox panted. His curly dark hair was damp with sweat. "I'm double-muscled!"

"Tell that to your mama," Apollo snarled.

"It's true," Joe said as he jogged beside them. "Lennox has the Hercules gene. It means he has muscles 25% larger and 50% stronger than an average human. If his bones were as strong, he could punch through a brick wall—"

"Save your breath for running, Joe," Apollo warned. "Strength without stamina is like a battle tank without fuel. Useless!"

They did ten minutes at full pelt on the treadmills and then Apollo shouted, "PRESS-UPS."

Troy was relieved just to get off his machine. He dropped to the floor and lay gasping for breath. From the other side of the room, Apollo counted out reps at top volume.

Troy was beginning to think that the crazy instructor could only shout, when Apollo spoke to him. "How many, Troy?"

"Errr ... none," he replied.

"NONE?" Apollo bellowed in fury. He moved to stand over Troy and re-started the count.

"One!"

Troy's arms shook as he raised himself off the floor.

"Two!"

Troy managed another press-up then collapsed. "I *can't* ... do any more," he wheezed. "I feel sick."

"I don't care if you vomit and have to dip your face in it," replied Apollo. "There's no *can't* in my gym. You won't stop until you sweat blood!"

Joe piped up. "That's not possible because—"

"Quit your science babble, Joe," Apollo snapped. "It's just a saying!"

He shook his head in despair at Troy's pathetic

attempt to do a third press-up. Seeing it was a lost cause, Apollo said, "OK, time to pound those punch bags before our new excuse for a recruit bursts a blood vessel."

The team jumped up and stood in front of a row of solid leather bags hanging on hooks from the ceiling.

"I want five 30-second rounds of jab-cross-jab," Apollo barked. "Starting now!"

As they punched the bags, he went on shouting. "In an attack situation, your first plan should be to escape with the VIP."

Troy jabbed his left fist at his bag. It was like punching cement.

"But if you have to confront the threat head-on," Apollo explained, "then punch to buy time. As soon as the way is clear, escape."

Troy threw his best effort at a cross. The bag barely twitched under the impact.

Apollo rolled his eyes in dismay. "That punch will buy you *zero* seconds! Put some power behind it, Troy. Hit it like you mean it! A bulletcatcher needs to build muscle memory so that your self-defence becomes second nature. JAB! CROSS! JAB!"

Troy pummelled the bag for all he was worth. His heart pounded in his chest. Sweat poured off him. His knuckles turned red raw. Then his wrist crumpled against the rock-solid bag and pain shot up his arm. But he kept going, terrified of Apollo's rage.

All of a sudden, a loud THUD in the gym brought everyone to a stop. Lennox had punched his bag so hard that it had flown off its hook and split. The bag lay on the floor like a gutted pig, its stuffing spilling out everywhere.

"Lennox, that's the third bag this month!" Apollo cried in irritation.

"It's not my fault they don't make them strong

enough," Lennox said. He tried to push the stuffing back in.

"Leave it!" Apollo snarled. "That's the warm-up done. Now we can begin the training session proper."

"Begin?" Troy exclaimed. He dropped to his knees with exhaustion. "I thought that *was* the training!"

8. ONE SECOND FIGHTING

"In a conflict situation," Apollo said, "you have 30 seconds *at most* to defeat your attacker."

Apollo had ignored Troy's pleading and Troy had dragged himself to his feet and joined Kasia and the others in a semi-circle on the padded mats of the dojo. This was Troy's first ever martial arts lesson. He had watched plenty of old samurai and ninja movies, but he had no idea what to expect from their fearsome instructor.

"It's a tactical error to think more time is going to help," Apollo went on. "First, the longer you spend fighting, the more the VIP is put at risk. Second, it's like trying to save yourself from drowning. If you can't do what you need to do in the first 30 seconds, more time will only make matters worse, not better. That's why you need to end the fight *fast* and *first*."

He beckoned Lennox to join him in the middle of the dojo.

"So today we'll go on with our *Kyusho Jitsu* training," Apollo said.

Troy turned to Azumi, who was still wearing her dark glasses. "What's *Kyusho Jitsu?*" he whispered to her.

"The ancient art of pressure-point fighting," she replied under her breath. "In English, *Kyusho Jitsu* means 'One Second Fighting'."

"You mean you can defeat someone in *one* second?" Troy exclaimed in disbelief.

"Pay attention!" Apollo turned with a sharp clap of his hands. "As I was saying, *Kyusho Jitsu* works by attacking the weaker points of the human body. For example ..." He strode over to Troy and raised a rock-hard fist. "If I was to give you a light punch in the head, it would have little effect."

Troy cowered from his instructor's threat – he didn't care how "light" the impact might be, he knew it would hurt.

"If I punched a bit harder, I might bruise your face," Apollo went on. "Harder again and you might stagger back or even be dazed. Full force, I'll probably break your nose and knock you out. But I might also damage my hand on your thick skull. So, what if ..."

Without warning, Apollo poked two fingers into Troy's eyes.

"Ow!" Troy cried. He jerked away and clasped a hand to his throbbing eyeballs. "What did you do that for?"

"To show you the principle of *Kyusho Jitsu*," Apollo said. It was clear he had no sympathy for Troy. "That attack was very light, but the result was dramatic. A big effect for a small amount of force. Do you understand now?"

Troy nodded his head. He didn't need another practical example.

"Good, lesson learned!" Apollo said, and he strode back over to Lennox. "We'll begin with pressure point ST-9."

Apollo placed a finger at the front of Lennox's neck, just to the right-hand side of his Adam's apple. "A strike to this point at the correct angle and force can stun and drop an attacker," he explained.

He gave Lennox's neck a light tap with the edge of his hand. Lennox collapsed to his knees as if he were a puppet and Apollo had cut his strings.

"As you can see, this is very effective," Apollo said as he pulled Lennox back to his feet. "Anything more than 10% power will knock a person out."

"I'd like to see *that*!" Kasia said with a cheeky grin.

"I'm sure you would," Apollo replied, and he narrowed his eyes. "But I want everyone to be extra careful working on this move. At full force it can kill. Now partner up."

Troy found himself opposite Lennox.

"Take it easy on him," Apollo warned Lennox. "Remember, he isn't a punch bag."

Troy looked over at the ripped leather bag lying on the floor and began to tremble at what lay in store for him.

Lennox smiled. "Don't worry, I'll be gentle," he promised as his hand connected with Troy's neck.

The jolt that raced through Troy's body felt like a tank hitting him. His legs buckled, his head buzzed and his vision went dark. The last thing he heard before he blacked out was Lennox insisting, "But I barely even touched him, *honest* ..."

9. MISSION PANDORA

One month later

Troy limped out of the Reactor Room.

"Congratulations!" Kasia said. She sat with her feet propped up on the control desk. "You lasted a full minute."

"One minute three seconds, in fact," Joe corrected her. He was studying the Reactor's feedback scores. "That equals a 6.3% daily increase in survival time, while your threat response has improved by 9.4% in the last 30 days."

"Great," Troy said. He hobbled over to a spare chair.

"Not really," Joe replied. "Your overall reaction

stats are still far too low. You've only got a 19% chance of surviving in any real-world attack."

"Thanks for the morale boost, Joe!" Troy sighed as he slumped into the seat with dismay.

His body hurt all over from combat training and now his leg was numb from where a reactor ball had struck him. Troy had discovered early on that being bulletproof didn't mean he was immune to pain. And the past month had been very long and very painful.

Every morning Troy asked himself if he'd been right to become a bulletcatcher. During the day he was tortured by fitness, martial arts and protection training – from bodycover tactics to foot formations to escape plans. In addition to those sessions, Medusa organised classes for them in threat assessment, mission planning, first aid, radio operation and surveillance detection. And all this was just scraping the surface of what a bulletcatcher needed to master. By the time Troy went to bed each night, his mind and body were burned out.

That said, he could now do 25 full press-ups before Apollo started shouting at him for slacking. There was enough power in his punches now that the bag sometimes swung like a pendulum after he'd hit it. And he knew where the ten most effective *Kyusho* points on the human body were. One of them, in fact, was the GB-31 nerve on the upper leg where the reactor ball had just hit him.

Troy tried to rub some life back into his numb thigh.

"Heads up!" Azumi said. "The Gorgon approaches."

She meant Medusa, who was named after the snake-haired, stony-gazed Gorgon of Greek myth. The control room door was closed, but Azumi still *knew* she was coming.

Troy wasn't surprised by this. Soon after he'd joined S.P.E.A.R., he'd discovered why Azumi wore dark glasses all the time. She was blind and her eyes were as white as milk. Yet Azumi considered herself blessed, since she had the talent of blindsight. Not only could she sense the world around her, enough to move freely and unaided in it, she had the power to glimpse into the future.

At breakfast one morning, Azumi had explained that her visions weren't 100% accurate. She only received brief images, sometimes just colours, and maybe no more than a feeling of threat. But, like a canary in a coal mine, she could warn that danger was near.

A moment later the control room door opened and Medusa popped her spiky head inside.

"Briefing room now," she ordered, and disappeared again.

Lennox punched the air in excitement. "We have a mission!"

The team ran out of the control room and into

the main chamber. As they took their seats, Medusa was already powering up the hologram desk.

"We've received reports that the Army of Freedom is planning an attack on the Council," she announced. "The A.F.'s target is Mayor Carlos Lomez and his daughter Pandora."

Two holographic images shimmered above the desk. One was a tall man with silver-grey hair, a tailored blue suit and movie-star looks. The second was a teenage girl with hazel eyes, braided hair and golden sun-kissed skin.

Lennox nudged Troy with his elbow. "She's even hotter than Reactor Room Jinx!"

Troy had to agree. As far as he could tell from the hologram, Pandora could be a supermodel, if she chose.

"Our mission is to protect Pandora at the opening of a new 'Fresh Air Park' in the Eastern Zone of the city," Medusa explained. The hologram

father and daughter were replaced by an interactive 3D map. Medusa pointed to a large green and blue dome among endless grey tower blocks. "Here's the park. Now, this is a public event, so we'll need to be on the look-out for *anything* unusual."

"Any intel on the type of threat we can expect?" Azumi asked.

Medusa shook her head. "The A.F.'s methods are hard to predict. It could be a gun assault, a bomb, a laser strike, a chemical attack or even a hoax. Whatever it turns out to be, our job is to keep Pandora safe."

Lennox put up his hand. "Can I be T.L. for this mission?"

"No, Kasia is team leader," Medusa replied. Lennox groaned with disappointment but she ignored him. "You, Joe and Azumi will form the defence ring around the VIP," she told him. "Troy will be the principal bulletcatcher."

"Me?" Troy exclaimed. "B ... but I'm not ready for a mission yet."

Medusa fixed him with her stone-grey eyes. "With your talent, you were born ready."

10. TATTOO

Troy stood beside Pandora as she greeted the cheering crowd in the Fresh Air Park. He kept to her right-hand side, about a metre back at all times. S.P.E.A.R. had taught him that this was the best position for a bulletcatcher – out of the VIP's personal space yet close enough to grab and shield them in the event of an attack.

Kasia and the rest of the team were dotted about in a loose circle, scanning the park for threats. Since they blended in with the other kids at the park opening, no one in the crowd paid them any heed.

Carlos Lomez walked into the park, stopping to shake hands with the cheering crowd. As the mayor and chairman of the Council he was a very powerful man, but despite this he was still pretty popular. His Fight Against Fear campaign had struck a chord with people who were worried about the rise of the A.F. and other terrorist groups. And his green policies were popular in a city choked with pollution. The new Fresh Air Park was a wonder. Under the 3-mile-wide dome was a paradise of green grass, tall trees, blue lakes and clean, fresh air.

"Troy, stay focused!" Kasia hissed in Troy's earpiece. "You should be watching the crowd, not Pandora!"

Troy blinked. He hadn't realised he was staring at her. Half an hour before, he'd been introduced to the mayor and his daughter. Shy as ever, Troy had been lost for words. Pandora had looked a bit worried.

"I thought my bulletcatcher would be ... bigger," she'd said, but then she'd put on a cheery smile and added, "Well, let's just hope nobody attacks us today, eh?"

Troy hadn't known how to respond, so he'd simply followed her like a faithful puppy dog.

He now focused on the task in hand and scanned the countless faces around Pandora – bright-eyed children, smiling mothers, excited teenagers and cheering fathers. Flashes from dozens of cameras blinded Troy as reporters jostled to get the best shot for that night's news. Cheering and clapping filled the air, adding to the confusion.

How was Troy supposed to spot a threat in such a huge crowd?

Then Troy caught a glimpse of shaved blond hair and a small black tattoo. His heart almost stopped in his chest. He could swear he'd just seen the terrorist from the shopping mall.

Or had he imagined it?

Almost every night, Troy relived his parents' brutal murder. He would wake in a fevered sweat from a nightmare in which a faceless tattooed monster chased him through a dark maze-like mall for hours until at last Troy felt the bullets rip into his back ...

Troy craned his neck to look for the man again, but the crowd had swallowed him up.

"I think I've seen an A.F. terrorist," he whispered into his mic. "The one that killed my parents."

"Where?" Kasia responded over the radio.

"To my right, 15 metres into the crowd," Troy replied.

"Draw closer, catchers," Kasia said, and the team tightened the defence ring around Pandora. "Do you sense anything, Azumi?"

"Negative," Azumi replied.

"Troy, what's the suspect's profile?" Lennox said.

"Blond hair. Heavy build. Tattoo behind his left ear," Troy told them.

"We'll need more than that to go on," Kasia said as she scanned the crowd.

"Describe the tattoo," said Joe.

"Err, it's ... like a stick man without a head," Troy said.

"The kanji symbol for fire," Joe said right away. "I saw that same tattoo earlier. The suspect is white, 1.85 metres, 86 kilos and in his mid-thirties. He's wearing sunglasses, a white cotton T-shirt and a heavy black jacket with a hood. I consider that weird on such a hot day, so the odds are he's carrying a weapon—"

"You heard Joe," Medusa interrupted. She was monitoring the situation from the mobile ops van. "Everyone, stay sharp."

Troy edged closer to Pandora as he looked for the terrorist among the crowd.

"Should we evac the VIP?" Lennox asked.

"Not yet," Medusa replied. "Do not act unless a real threat is identified. A false alarm could be embarrassing for the mayor, as well as S.P.—"

"Code Red!" Azumi cut in over the radio. "I've had a vision."

"Any details?" Kasia asked.

"No," Azumi said. "Just a purple colour. I think someone intends to attack."

"I can't see him," Troy said, and his voice shook with panic. "Where's he gone? He's disap—"

All of a sudden, a woman pushed to the front of the crowd and hurled a grenade at Pandora. Troy saw it fly through the air. He froze in terror as the lethal device dropped towards Pandora.

Troy was bulletproof, not bomb proof!

At the last split-second, Kasia stepped in and pulled Pandora clear. Joe, Azumi and Lennox all piled on top to shield her from the blast. The grenade struck Troy in the chest. The casing shattered, splattering black liquid all over his T-shirt.

The Council's security force went into overdrive.

"CHEM ATTACK!" one of the bodyguards

shouted. He grabbed the mayor and rushed him over to a limo that was waiting on stand-by.

As the crowd panicked and screamed, two security guards tackled the woman who'd thrown the grenade. Kasia and the rest of the team bundled Pandora into a second limo and shot off at high speed.

Troy looked down at his chest and was amazed he was still alive. At last he snapped out of his daze and sprinted after them. But an Emergency Response Squad in full-body yellow protective suits appeared and blocked his path.

"*Halt!*" they ordered, and Troy was forced to the ground at gunpoint.

11. HERO GENE

"You were lucky, Troy, that woman was a protester and *not* a terrorist," Medusa said. They were having a team debrief back at S.P.E.A.R. HQ. "You're even luckier that the 'grenade' was only a water bomb filled with ink. That's why the body scanners at the park gate didn't pick it up."

Troy didn't feel very lucky. He'd been held at gunpoint, stripped naked and his skin had been rubbed raw in case the black liquid was a chemical weapon, and only then did they discover it was harmless black ink! Yet Kasia and the others were still sitting a few seats away from him just to be safe.

"The mayor sends his heartfelt thanks to you all for protecting his daughter," Medusa went on.

"He's requested our services again for the Council's annual charity ball next weekend."

A glittering globe with the red C logo of the Council hovered above the hologram desk.

"That's the most secure event of the year," Kasia said. "Why does he need us?"

"Because of the terrorist Troy saw at the park today, we suspect that the A.F. did intend to launch an attack," Medusa explained. "But the protester struck first and disrupted their plans. Which means they will try again."

Medusa closed down the hologram desk and walked up the stairs to the upper gallery. At the exit, she paused and turned to them. "Good work, catchers," she said. "And that was heroic of you, Troy, to stand and take the attack head-on."

As the door slid shut behind her, a heavy silence fell over the chamber. Troy sensed everyone's eyes upon him.

"That's not how I remember it," Kasia said. Her snow-white face was flushed with anger. "What happened to you at the park, Troy?"

"He had brain fade," Joe said. "It's a natural response to an attack – fight, flight or freeze. He froze."

"Well, you *can't* freeze if you're a bulletcatcher," said Kasia.

"I'm no bulletcatcher," Troy replied. His voice came out flat and he couldn't meet Kasia's eye.

"Too right you're not!" Kasia said. "I had to cover for you. You failed to react and put Pandora and the rest of the team at risk."

"Don't be so hard on him," Azumi said. "We all make mistakes."

"Yeah, it's just first-time nerves," said Lennox. "Remember, he saved that girl back in the shopping mall. He'll be fine next ti—"

Troy interrupted him. "No, I didn't," he said.

"What do you mean?" said Lennox.

"I tried to tell Medusa, but she wouldn't listen," Troy explained. "I was running for the exit when ... well ... my foot slipped on a comic and I fell on top of the girl. It was by accident."

Kasia and the others stared at him in disbelief.

"Of course I'm glad the girl survived, but I *didn't* try to save her," Troy admitted. "I was trying to save my own skin." He hung his head in shame. "I'm no hero. I'm a coward."

"I knew you were too good to be true," Kasia said. Her voice was harsh with contempt. "You're a danger to us, Troy. *You* might be bulletproof, but the rest of us aren't!"

With that, she stormed up the stairs and disappeared into the Rec Room.

Azumi followed Kasia. But as she passed Troy, she rested a hand on his arm. "We all have talents for a reason," she said. "You just need to find your reason."

Lennox shrugged. "Hey, I don't know why Kasia's making such a big thing of it. No one died. See you at dinner, Troy."

He bounded up the steps two at a time. Troy was left alone with Joe. He held his head in his hands and stared at the floor. "I may be bulletproof," he said, "but that doesn't mean I have some hero gene!"

"You're right," Joe said. "*You* don't have one."

"Thanks a lot," said Troy. "You're a real help."

"I try to be," Joe said. He put on a smile. "Listen," he said. "I've seen the CCTV film of the mall attack. It was logical for you to run. You didn't know about your bulletproof talent. Without it, there was less than a 5% chance you could save the girl."

"That's enough, Joe!" Troy snapped. "I don't need any more of your statistics. Just leave me alone, will you? What do you know anyway?"

"Everything," Joe replied. "My talent is recall. In truth, it's just one of my many talents. I can also do advanced computer programming, mathematics and play piano to concert standard. I am also autistic. Autism used to be called a disability, but I consider it an advantage. I have a photographic memory and instant recall. I can speed-read at an amazing rate and retain 98% of the information."

Troy shook his head in confusion. "What are you trying to say, Joe?" he asked.

"There is no single gene that makes someone a hero," Joe said. "If you study history, most heroes are normal people. It's the heroic *act* that's special."

"Well, I *didn't* act." Troy sighed. He sank down in his chair as the sense of his own shame crushed him.

"No, you didn't," said Joe. "But you will act next time. You may be a bulletcatcher but you don't need a special talent to be a hero."

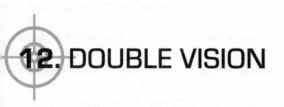12. DOUBLE VISION

The ballroom in Terminus City's old opera house was filled with the rich and famous. Politicians, movie stars and energy tycoons mingled with TV personalities, pop stars and supermodels. On the stage a band played old-time jazz, while guests sipped Champagne from neon-lit glasses that changed colour in time with the music. Floating tables served lobster, caviar, quail jelly and a whole roast pig – food Troy had never laid eyes upon before, let alone tasted for real.

The glamorous room and lavish food was the high standard people expected at Terminus City's most exclusive event of the year. But in the midst of all this glitz, the centre of attention was Pandora.

Dressed in a sparkling jumpsuit and a pair of diamond earrings, she was the talk of the party. And with so many people trying to get near her, Troy had his work cut out to spot any potential threats.

As Troy scanned the crowd over and over, he felt as taut as a loaded spring. His nerves were on a razor's edge. After his chat with Joe, he was no longer scared of an attack. He was scared he wouldn't react in time and so might risk the team's lives again ... and Pandora's.

There was a lull in the stream of guests, and Pandora turned to Troy.

"I haven't had the chance to thank you," she whispered. "I'm sorry I was rude about your ability to protect me. You did a great job."

Troy responded with an awkward smile. "It was Kasia who *really* saved you."

Pandora raised an eyebrow. "You're very humble, Troy. I like that."

Troy felt his cheeks redden at the compliment, even if he didn't deserve it.

"I also like the fact you don't talk too much," she added. "The boys I know just go on about themselves all the time. Of course, they just want to impress me because of who I am. You're not like that, Troy."

Pandora graced him with one of her dazzling smiles and then she wandered off into the crowd. Troy followed a few discreet steps behind, yet close enough to intervene if he was needed. In a social situation like this one, the guests had been checked by security guards with body scanners at the door and that meant Troy didn't need to be right beside his VIP at all times.

Troy watched Pandora greet each person in turn as she made them laugh and asked them to dig deep into their pockets for the charity auction. He wondered why anyone would want to hurt her in the first place.

A young model in a gold sequin dress shimmied up to him. "Aren't you that mystery boy on the news?" she said with a sweet smile. "The one who saved Pandora?"

When Troy didn't reply, she took that as a yes.

"I'm Tabitha," she said, and she rested a hand on his arm. "So, what's your name?"

"Troy," he managed to reply.

Typical! he thought. He'd never had any luck with girls, but now he seemed to have become a magnet for them. Perhaps there was some benefit to being a bulletcatcher after all! But as pretty as this girl Tabitha was, Troy knew that he couldn't allow himself to become distracted.

"Sorry, I've got to go," he said. He offered her a polite smile and then followed Pandora across the ballroom.

"Catch you later," Tabitha said with a playful wink.

Lennox's voice sounded in Troy's ear. "Did you get her number, Romeo?"

"No," Troy said as he took up guard near Pandora again. "Where are you?"

"By the food, of course." Lennox chuckled. "The lobster is amazing—"

"Stop thinking with your stomach, Lennox," Kasia cut in. "You're not here to enjoy yourself."

Troy spotted Kasia off to his left. She was studying one of the artworks up for auction – a tall glass sculpture of a breaking wave – but Troy knew that she was really watching the ballroom in its reflection. As he passed her, Kasia refused to make eye contact. Even after a week, she was still angry with him.

"Any sign of your terrorist yet?" she demanded through her mic.

"Negative," he replied.

"Joe, how about you?" she asked.

Joe stood near the stage, where he appeared to be listening to the band. "So far I've spotted three men with the same build and height as our suspect," he said. "But none have blond hair or a visible tattoo."

"Maybe the A.F. have been scared off by all the security?" Lennox said.

"Don't speak too soon," said Azumi. "I've just had a vision – a knife."

Troy eyed the people near Pandora. "I see no threat."

"Nor do I," said Kasia.

"Azumi, you must be sensing the chef's knife," Lennox said. "He's about to carve up the pig."

A bearded man in a chef's hat stood over the hog roast, sharpening a long blade.

"No," Azumi responded. "I'm seeing a lot of red. Someone is very angry."

As Azumi spoke, the sound of raised voices

came from the other side of the room. An elegant red-haired woman threw a glass of Champagne into a man's face, then stormed off.

"False alarm," Lennox said.

Then Troy spotted a waiter with short blond hair heading for Pandora.

"Maybe not," he said. He moved fast to cut the man off. "Suspect waiter at 12 o'clock!"

He was about to confront the suspect, when Kasia cried out, "It's not him. It's your model in the gold dress!"

Troy spun to see Tabitha make a beeline for Pandora. There was a glint of steel in her hand. Kasia shot forward with the speed of an arrow and struck the girl in the neck at the ST-9 pressure point. Tabitha crumpled to the polished wooden floor of the ballroom.

"Something's still wrong," Azumi said. "I'm getting a double vision. There's a gun this time."

That's when Troy saw the chef slice open the belly of the pig and pull out the pistol that was hidden inside.

13. SACRIFICE

For a moment, time seemed to slow. He saw everything in great detail as if he had Kasia's reflex talent.

The ceramic gun that would have escaped the security metal detectors ...

The calm way the chef took aim at Pandora ...

The tell-tale twitch of a muscle as the chef pulled the gun's trigger ...

Troy wasn't even aware that he'd dived into the line of fire. It was pure instinct.

The bullet meant for Pandora struck Troy in the chest like a battering ram. Then the force rippled across his skin, spreading the lethal energy and

saving him from harm. Winded from the impact, Troy hit the ground hard.

The chef swore in anger and fired again just as Lennox shoved the entire floating table of roast pig into him. The chef was thrown back against the wall. His aim was knocked off and his hat fell to one side to reveal short blond hair and the kanji fire tattoo.

The second bullet whistled past Pandora, missing her by a fraction and hitting the wave sculpture instead. The priceless artwork exploded, sending fragments of glass flying across the ballroom floor. Screams filled the air and guests began to run in all directions. Kasia and Azumi seized Pandora and rushed her towards the exit.

Lennox made a grab for the chef. He got a handful of his beard, but the chef ripped his head away and fled out the swing doors into the kitchen.

Troy was reeling from the impact of the bullet

but still very much alive. He staggered to his feet and ran after the terrorist.

"Where are you going?" Lennox shouted. He was still holding the chef's false beard in his hand.

Troy clutched a hand to his bruised chest and gasped, "To catch my parents' killer."

He sprinted into the kitchen, but he couldn't see the terrorist anywhere.

"Troy, there's only one exit," Joe said over his earpiece. "Far right, to the back."

Troy spotted a door swinging shut. He ran over, burst into a stairwell and glimpsed a figure running upwards.

Racing after the suspect, he took the steps two at time. He was grateful now for Apollo's painful fitness sessions.

Above him, he heard a door slam. Five flights later, Troy reached the top of the stairs where a fire door led onto the roof of the opera house. He shoved it open with his shoulder and burst out into a neon-lit night.

The blond-haired terrorist was waiting for him, with the gun primed in his hand.

Troy was blown off his feet by a second bullet.

"You don't die easily, do you?" the terrorist said as he stood over Troy's body.

Behind the man's back, Troy could see the lights of a heli-plane coming in to land. The terrorist raised his hand and signalled to the pilot.

"Why ... did you kill my parents?" Troy groaned.

The terrorist cocked his head to one side. "Did I?"

"At the mall. You shot them."

"In a war for freedom, sacrifices must be made," the terrorist replied. He pointed his gun at Troy's head. "No sacrifice, no victory."

With a squeeze of the trigger, he shot Troy point blank.

Troy fell still.

He was out cold for a good ten seconds. Then, as if emerging from a free dive deep into the sea, Troy came back to life. He saw the heli-plane making its final approach. In a last attempt to stop the terrorist escaping, Troy leaped up and punched the man's thigh with all his might.

His knuckles struck the pressure point he had aimed for.

The terrorist's leg crumpled under him. As he tried to shoot Troy again, Troy targeted the man's upper arm at pressure point P-2. The terrorist cried out in agony and dropped his gun.

Troy snatched it up.

"Are *you* willing to make the ultimate sacrifice?" Troy said. He aimed the gun and put his finger on the trigger.

"Of course," the terrorist replied. He smiled as he held up his hands in surrender. "But you have to understand I'm just the weapon. You should be asking yourself, who is *really* pulling the trigger?"

A gunshot rang out and the terrorist slumped at Troy's feet with a bullet in his heart.

From the roof of the opera house, Troy watched the heli-plane disappear into the night.

14. BULLETCATCHER

"Well done, bulletcatchers!" Medusa said as she entered the Rec Room at S.P.E.A.R. HQ the next morning.

Troy and the rest of the team were shattered from the events of the night before. They lay sprawled in the GameChairs, sipping energy smoothies for breakfast.

"Mayor Lomez is deeply grateful for our services," Medusa went on. "And Pandora has asked that Troy become her permanent bulletcatcher from now on."

Lennox elbowed Troy in the ribs and grinned. "You lucky git!"

"Doesn't matter how hot the VIP is, I'm not

so lucky if she's getting shot at all the time," Troy replied. His head was still throbbing and his chest still hurt from where the bullets had hit him.

"I should hope that now your terrorist is dead," Medusa said, "the A.F. will think twice before they attack the mayor's daughter again, or anyone else in the Council for that matter." She turned her stone-grey eyes on Kasia. "Oh, and you'll be pleased to know, Kasia, that the model you knocked out cold *isn't* planning to make a complaint."

Then Medusa turned on her heels and left the room.

"Why's she blaming me?" Kasia complained. "So the model wasn't a terrorist. But what sort of idiot carries a make-up mirror shaped like a dagger?"

"It was my fault really," Azumi said. "The double vision confused me."

"We *all* make mistakes," Troy said, remembering that Azumi had used the same words the week before.

Kasia sighed. "I suppose so. I'm sorry I ever doubted you, Troy."

"Now you're a real hero," Joe said. He looked up from the gadget he was programming. "Not just a hero by accident."

Troy laughed. "You don't half have a way with words, Joe."

Troy reached into his pocket and pulled out the photo of his parents. He hoped they would be proud of him and he prayed their spirits could find peace now that their murderer was dead.

Lennox leaned over and whispered. "What I want to know is, did *you* kill that terrorist?"

Troy shook his head. "No, that wasn't me. I'm not a killer. I'm a *bulletcatcher.*"

Part 2

Sniper

15. GLINT OF SUNLIGHT

Troy waited like a patient boyfriend as Pandora browsed the racks of glamorous dresses. But he had little hope that he would ever be the sweetheart of this beauty with her raven hair and honey skin. Pandora was the daughter of Carlos Lomez, the mayor of Terminus City and the chairman of the all-powerful Council. She was way out of Troy's league.

His job was to protect her.

Troy's gaze swept round the designer fashion store. Among the customers he spotted an ice-blonde girl. She appeared to be looking at a silk top. In fact, her sharp blue eyes were watching the other shoppers.

Kasia was a bulletcatcher like Troy, assigned to guard Pandora.

Outside the shop a large boy loitered, with arms like blocks of black granite. That was Lennox – the muscle on their team.

There was no sign of any threat. Even so, Troy felt on edge. He'd hated shopping malls ever since his parents were killed in one in a terrorist attack. Over a year had passed, but the grief still burned like acid in his gut.

As he kept a look-out for danger, Troy caught sight of his own reflection in a mirror. Tall and pale with sandy cropped hair, he looked a little gawky. But he was no longer the scrawny boy he once was. After months of intensive bulletcatcher training, his body was stronger and more defined.

"What do you think of this one?" Pandora asked. She held a ruby-red dress against her slim figure.

Troy stared at her. His confidence was growing,

but he was still tongue-tied when it came to girls. Especially one as pretty as Pandora. "Ermm ... very nice," he said.

Pandora smiled. "You've said that about *all* the clothes I've shown you."

She paid for the dress and several other items, then strolled out of the store. Lennox walked ahead and took "point". Troy kept close on Pandora's right. Kasia followed behind on their left. In this way, Pandora was protected from all sides.

"Heading to north exit," Kasia whispered into her throat mic.

Troy heard a reply in their earpieces from Joe, their comms contact at S.P.E.A.R. HQ. "Transport ETA one minute," Joe said.

Troy's nerves grew worse. Whenever a VIP got in or out of a vehicle, they were vulnerable. This was the moment they were most exposed to a potential attack.

Pandora and her bulletcatchers reached the exit as the limo pulled up to the kerb outside.

The mall's glass doors slid open. Lennox stepped onto the street and did a quick scan. His eyes lingered on a man talking into a mobile before he gave the all-clear.

Troy escorted Pandora across the pavement. Lennox opened the limo's rear door. As Troy guided Pandora towards it, his eyes darted everywhere for threats. The man with the mobile had finished his call and was walking towards them. Kasia stepped forward and blocked his path. The man may have been innocent, but they couldn't take any chances.

Pandora was totally unaware of the threat as she slipped into the back seat with her shopping bags.

"Well, that was easy," Lennox said with a grin. He had begun to close the door when the limo's front tyre burst. "Oh hell!" he said. "We've got a flat—"

Troy looked up. His eyes were drawn by a glint of sunlight from the roof of a building further along the street. Suddenly Lennox gave a wounded cry and keeled over.

At that moment, Pandora climbed back out. "I've forgotten my purse," she said.

"No!" Troy cried as she left the safety of the vehicle.

Troy leaped forward to cover Pandora with his body. He felt a bullet strike his back. Then another. The impacts knocked the air from his lungs. He hit the pavement hard.

A second later, Pandora fell beside him. A bullet in her head.

16. BULLET EARS

Troy stared into Pandora's dead eyes. Despair welled up in him. He'd *failed* to protect her.

Pandora's face flickered. Then blinked out.

The street scene and limo also vanished to reveal a huge round room with a domed roof. The walls glowed soft white and a faint hum could be heard. The Reactor Room simulation was over.

Troy recovered his breath then got to his feet. He entered the control room with Kasia and a dazed Lennox.

"Lucky you're bulletproof," Azumi said to Troy. Her long black hair was tied into a ponytail and her eyes were hidden behind a pair of sunglasses.

"Yeah, *he's* bulletproof," Lennox moaned. He

rubbed the back of his head where one of the rubber bullets had hit him. "But I'm not!"

"You're super-strong. You can take it." Kasia laughed.

Lennox narrowed his eyes at her. "How come you didn't get shot?"

"Reflex, baby, reflex," she replied with a wink.

Each of the team had been signed up by S.P.E.A.R. – a top secret protection agency – because of their unique talents. Troy was bulletproof. Lennox had the Hercules gene that made him 50% stronger than even the strongest adult. Azumi had blindsight that allowed her to glimpse into the future and warn of danger. Kasia's reflex talent meant she could react six times faster than any normal human.

Before Lennox could sit down, Kasia claimed the only other chair in the room.

"Too slow!" She laughed as she propped her feet on the control desk and leaned back.

Joe tutted and pushed her feet off so he could study the screen's read-outs. He was a skinny boy with square glasses that suited a tech-head.

"So how did we do?" Kasia asked as she put her feet back on the desk.

Joe looked up at her and frowned. "Your VIP is dead. You failed."

"We know *that*," Kasia replied breezily. "But did we get any points?"

"Points are pointless if your VIP is killed," Joe said. Still, he examined the read-out. "The team was scoring well at first: 98% for surveillance skills in the clothes store; 95% for the walking drill; 62% for street observation; 30% for transfer into the limo—"

"Why the sudden drop in our scores?" Troy asked.

"None of you looked *up* as you moved the VIP from the mall to the limo. You all focused on the obvious threat – the man in the street. Then you dropped your guard as soon as Pandora was in the car. So you missed the sniper on the roof."

Troy recalled the glint of sunlight. That must have been from the scope on the sniper's rifle!

"But how are we supposed to spot a sniper?" Lennox complained.

"You can't," Joe replied. "That's what makes them so deadly."

Lennox threw his hands up in the air. "So we had no chance!"

"Not really," Joe said. "Snipers use camouflage, choose a firing position with care and often attack from long distances. It's only *after* a sniper has taken their first shot that you have any chance of locating them. Of course, it's often too late by then."

"Are you saying we can't *ever* stop a sniper?" Kasia asked.

Joe pulled up an image on the computer screen of a large mast with an array of sensors. "This is a Boomerang device. A military system that uses microphones to calculate the sniper's position from the muzzle blast and the bullet's sonic shock-wave. But the device needs to be mounted to a vehicle, costs a lot and weighs a ton. The other option is a dog."

"Really?" Azumi said. She looked thoughtful.

Joe nodded. "Trained dogs can work out the direction of the sniper from the sound of the bullet. In the Vietnam War, one famous dog located over one hundred enemy snipers by lying down with his head pointed at the origin of the gunshot. They nicknamed him Bullet Ears."

"Shame none of us are dogs, huh?" Lennox said.

"Speak for yourself," Kasia joked. "You smell like one!"

Lennox wrinkled his nose in mock offence. "If that's the case, then you'd be a Husky! And Azumi would be a Pekingese."

"I'm from Japan, not China, Dog-breath!" Azumi shot back.

"Whatever," Lennox said with a shrug. "Troy's from Poland and he'd still be a tiny Shih Tzu!"

"That's lame, Lennox," Troy replied. He turned to Joe. "So what are our best tactics to deal with a sniper?"

"Obviously if you're still alive, take cover," Joe replied. "Next, escape the kill-zone as fast as you can. But the best defence is to prevent it ever happening. A security team should sweep the area in advance. Then you should post guards on all rooftops and tall buildings. The more eyes and ears the better. But that takes a lot of resources, both in terms of money and manpower."

Troy shook his head in amazement. "How do you know all this?" he asked.

Joe gave him a puzzled look. "I've told you before, I retain 98% of everything I see and read thanks to my—"

Troy held up a hand and smiled. "Yeah, I know, your autistic superpowers!"

The door to the control room slid open and a woman appeared. She had spiked white hair and a silver-grey suit. Medusa was the head of S.P.E.A.R. and the severe look on her face told them she had bad news.

"The sniper's struck again."

# 17. THE JUDGE

A short woman with a brown bob and sturdy shoes strode out of the new hospital. As she waved goodbye to the crowd, her body jerked and she fell to the ground. Blood spread in a large red pool around her head.

Troy watched the replay of the attack in mute horror. The other bulletcatchers also sat stunned in the large round briefing chamber as the hologram desk zoomed in on the scene.

"Anna Kerner is the *third* member of the Council to be killed in as many months," the newsreader said. "It seems Terminus City is no longer safe for anyone."

The camera switched to the TV studio, where

the blonde newsreader sat with the stern-faced Head of Council Security.

"Are your security forces failing us, Commander Hanz?" the newsreader asked.

"Of course not!" the commander snapped. "For the hospital's opening ceremony, we had police stationed for a three-block radius."

He stabbed a finger at the area lit up in green on a digital map of the city.

"The sniper was beyond this zone, hidden in a radio tower."

A red dot glowed near the edge of the map.

"Only one in a million could have made such a shot," the commander said. "No one could have foreseen or prevented such an attack. We're up against a professional sniper. We suspect he's ex-elite forces."

With a grim nod the newsreader turned to the camera. "This is a worrying development in our battle against the terrorists. Once again the Army of

Freedom have claimed responsibility for this latest attack in an online video by their leader, The Judge."

The newscast switched to a man in a robe and a Janus mask – a half black, half white face that was both smiling and crying.

"I am your judge, jury and executioner," the masked man said in a rasping voice. "Terminus City is immoral. The Council is corrupt. The mayor is a thief and liar."

He held up a small wooden hammer to the camera. "The sentence is death!"

He brought the hammer down onto its wooden block with a sharp *crack*.

The Judge went on. "My Army of Freedom will tear this city down and rebuild it in the name of God." He turned his head so only the smile showed. "Be faithful and you will live." Then he twisted to show the single black tear on the other side. "But all non-believers and sinners will die."

Troy's stomach knotted in anger at The Judge's words. His parents *hadn't* been non-believers or sinners. They were good people. Innocent. Just living their lives. Their only crime was to be shopping at the time of the mall attack when these terrorists gunned them down in cold blood.

Their deaths were the reason Troy was now a bulletcatcher.

He'd never imagined or wanted to be a bodyguard. He wasn't a natural hero – not like Kasia. But he'd been forced into the role by all that had happened. And, having watched The Judge's video, Troy was more determined than ever to stop the terrorists and their insane crusade.

The video was followed by a news clip of a tanned man with dark eyebrows, a square jaw and silver-grey hair. The calm and determined face of Mayor Lomez.

"We will *not* be terrorised by the A.F.," the

mayor said, and he pounded a fist on his lectern.
"The Judge's threats do not scare me. And they
should not scare you. Together we will Fight Against
Fear."

The mayor pointed to a banner with the words
Fight Against Fear etched on a shield.

"The Council has already agreed tighter
security measures," Mayor Lomez went on. "One
hundred more city drones will fly the skies. Thirty
more armed police units will patrol the streets.
Online surveillance will be extended. There'll be
no rock, roof or computer these terrorists can hide
behind."

He stared direct into the camera lens. "As your
mayor, I promise to keep this city safe from these
faceless terrorists."

Medusa switched off the hologram desk and
turned to Troy and the others.

"Well, that speech should guarantee him

another four years as mayor," she said, then raised a thin eyebrow. "Which means he and his daughter will continue to be the prime target for the A.F. Your role as bulletcatchers is more vital than ever."

18. ZANSHIN ZONE

"I'm dying!" Troy gasped.

"QUIT MOANING!" Apollo barked. Their fitness and combat instructor was a six-foot-two mountain of bad-tempered muscle and the only help he gave Troy was to shout, "PAIN IS TEMPORARY!"

Troy lugged the heavy medicine ball to the far end of the gym for the tenth time. His legs trembled beneath him, his arms ached and his heart threatened to burst out of his ribs. Even Fit Pills were no help under training this intense.

"Next station!" Apollo ordered.

Troy dropped the medicine ball with a *thud*, staggered across to a mat and began to do a combination of press-ups, star jumps and burpees.

Lennox jogged past him with Joe on his back. He was sweating buckets.

"I'm melting," Lennox complained as he completed another circuit of the gym.

"Sweat is just your fat crying!" Apollo replied, and made as if to kick him in the rear. "Get moving!"

Lennox stumbled on. When someone as strong as Lennox was struggling, Troy realised he had little chance. With every star jump, he was feeling more and more light-headed.

"Your talents may give you the edge in an attack, but they won't guarantee your VIP's survival ... or your own!" Apollo said as he added extra weight to Kasia's bench press. "No point having superpowers if you're not in the right place at the right time. That's why you must be fighting fit!"

Then he increased the resistance on Azumi's cycling machine and shouted at her to go faster.

"There are three factors that determine your

speed to an attack situation," Apollo explained. "Reaction, response and rapidity. The Reactor Room can improve reaction and response times. But only hard work in the gym will improve rapidity. This is how swift your muscles contract, how quick your counter punch is, and how fast your body moves out of the way of danger."

Without warning, Apollo swung a sledgehammer fist at Troy and caught him in the gut. Troy dropped to the mat, where he fought for breath.

"Troy, you may be able to stop a bullet, but you couldn't stop my fist!" Apollo snarled with a disappointed shake of his bald head.

Tears of pain stung Troy's eyes. "*Why ... did you ... hit me?*" he groaned.

Apollo smiled. "I've just taught you a very valuable lesson. Action beats reaction every single time. Don't just stand there and wait for someone to hit you – *move*."

"But ..." Troy gasped, "how could I know you'd punch me?"

Apollo jerked him to his feet. "You should have been in the Zanshin Zone."

"Zanshin?" Kasia asked. She parked her weights and sat up on the bench with a puzzled frown.

Apollo rolled his eyes. "Azumi, educate these fools."

Azumi stopped cycling. "Zanshin ... refers to a warrior's awareness," she panted. "It literally means *remaining mind*."

"And, as bulletcatchers, you need to be mindful at all times," Apollo said. "Mindful of your potential enemies and surroundings. There's an old samurai warrior saying – *When the battle is over, keep one hand on your sword*."

"But I don't have a sword," Lennox pointed out as he lowered Joe to the ground.

"Why am I not surprised *you* don't understand?"

Apollo growled. "The saying reminds you to stay alert at the end of any combat. It's natural to think the danger is over then – when in reality, it's often not."

All of a sudden Apollo pulled out a handgun and aimed it at Troy's head.

This time Troy did react. For the past month their instructor had been drilling them in gun-disarming techniques until they were second nature. Troy slammed one hand against the gun's barrel and chopped the other into Apollo's wrist, breaking his instructor's grip on the weapon.

The gun still went off, but the bullet missed Troy.

"Good reactions, Troy," Apollo said with a nod of approval. "Shame you killed Kasia in the process."

Troy turned to see Kasia fuming at him, with her ice-blue eyes ablaze. The paintball bullet had plastered her snow-white skin and platinum-blonde hair bright red.

"Sorry," he said with a sheepish grin.

19. FUNFAIR

"Step up! Test your strength!" the showman called. He beckoned to Troy and the others to try the High Striker.

Pandora had been invited to the city's annual summer funfair by Jeff, the son of Councillor Drayton. The whole family was there. The boy's father was proudly wearing a straw panama hat and was accompanied by several armed bodyguards in black combat gear.

Compared to these hulking security men, Troy and the other bulletcatchers could walk alongside Pandora undetected. No different to the other kids enjoying the old-fashioned funfair.

There were bumper cars, merry-go-rounds,

a helter-skelter, a big wheel, side stalls, candy floss and swarms of kids screaming in delight on the thrill-rides. With all the distractions, lights and noise, it was a nightmare location to protect someone.

"Come on! Let's sort the men from the boys!" the showman challenged. "Who's going to impress this pretty little lady here?" He shot a wink at Pandora.

Jeff stepped forward, handed the showman a credit and picked up the wooden mallet. He flicked his mop of ash-blond hair from his eyes, then said to Pandora, "Check this out."

Jeff swung the mallet down hard onto the striker pad. The puck flew up the tower ... but stopped short of the bell.

"Better luck next time!" the showman said with a toothy grin. "Want to try again?"

"Nah," Jeff said. Troy could tell by the boy's

sulky tone that he was annoyed at failing in front of Pandora.

"How about you, big man?" the showman said to Lennox.

Lennox shrugged. "OK."

He took the mallet in one hand and hit the striker with no more effort than if he were swatting a fly. The puck shot up like a rocket and the bell rang out.

The showman's jaw fell open in shock. "We've a real-life superman here!"

"Impressive," Pandora said. She smiled at Lennox as he claimed his prize of a furry toy gorilla.

Jeff scowled. "Well, he's got a lot more weight behind him, hasn't he?"

For a moment Lennox looked like he might use the mallet on Jeff.

"How about a different game?" Kasia suggested to defuse the tension. She guided the group towards a side stall.

"Yeah," Jeff said, regaining his confidence. "I'll win you a teddy bear, Pandora."

Jeff pushed into the crowd and headed for the shooting gallery. Troy wasn't warming to the boy. Jeff was rude, arrogant, brash and didn't seem to like Troy standing so close to Pandora all the time.

"Aren't you having a go?" Pandora asked Troy.

Troy shook his head. He couldn't allow himself to become distracted. He had to stay in the Zanshin Zone and keep an eye out for danger.

"Scared of guns, are we?" Jeff teased Troy as he paid the operator.

"I'll have a go," Azumi volunteered.

The operator handed her the rifle. "Ladies first," he said.

"Is this a good idea?" Lennox whispered to Troy. "Giving her a loaded weapon!"

Azumi seemed unfazed by the challenge. She pointed the rifle down the range at the tower of six tin cans on a shelf. She clicked her tongue once then pulled the trigger.

The top can flew off. Troy and Lennox exchanged astonished looks.

Another tongue click, a gunshot and the second can toppled.

As the third can went flying, Jeff asked Joe, "What's with the click?"

"Azumi is blind," Joe replied. "The click helps her echo-locate the target."

Jeff narrowed his eyes at Joe as Azumi shot a fourth can off. "You're pulling my leg."

"No, I'm not," Joe replied with a frown. "My hands are in my pockets."

Jeff looked at Joe as if he was deeply weird, then turned back to the shooting gallery. Azumi had missed the last two cans.

"Aww, unlucky," the operator said with a half-hearted shrug as he re-set the cans.

"Something's wrong," Azumi said. There was a frown on her face.

"Yeah, the sights on these are usually off," Jeff replied as he took the rifle from her. "You have to compensate."

Jeff raised the rifle and took careful aim. As he fired away, Troy couldn't deny he was an excellent shot. Jeff hit each can dead-centre and they pinged off the shelf like shooting stars. When the last can went flying, he punched the air and shouted, "Beat that!"

The operator reluctantly handed over a super-sized teddy bear clutching a red heart. Jeff presented the prize to Pandora with a smug smile.

"Thanks," she said, and hugged the bear to her chest.

"Sharpest shooter in Terminus City!" Jeff boasted. He closed one eye and took aim with the gun at his father, who was buying a stick of candy floss for his little sister. "I reckon I could knock that daft hat off his head from here."

"Something's definitely wrong," Azumi repeated as Jeff made a shooting sound. But not only did his father's hat go flying, his father dropped to the ground. Blood spurted from a bullet wound in his neck.

Jeff's face went pale. "But I didn't even pull the trigger!" he cried.

Troy knew in an instant Jeff *wasn't* to blame.

"CODE RED!" he shouted. "SNIPER!"

20. BAIT

Kasia reacted first. She shoved Pandora aside. Not a second too late.

A bullet ripped through the head of the teddy bear she was holding. Stuffing exploded into the air like snowflakes.

The bullet carried on and hit Jeff. He doubled over, clutching his bleeding belly, and screamed. Troy shielded Pandora with his body and rushed her into the cover of the shooting gallery. They huddled there with Kasia, Lennox, Joe and Azumi all forming a protective shield around Pandora.

"Where's the sniper?" Kasia said.

"I've no idea," Troy replied. His eyes darted from the big wheel to the bumper cars to the helter-skelter. Families and children still strolled around the funfair, unaware of the attack.

Jeff dropped to his knees, his screams lost among the joyful cries of the kids on the rides.

"Save my Jeffrey!" Troy heard Jeff's mother wail. She cowered behind the candy-floss stall with her daughter clasped in her arms, her dead husband only a few metres from her.

Jeff collapsed and one of the armed bodyguards rushed out to drag him to safety. As he reached the boy, a gunshot rang out. The bodyguard was blown off his feet, dead before he even hit the ground.

Now people began to notice the three bullet-stricken bodies. Panic spread like a tidal wave through the funfair. The chaos made it even more difficult to lead Pandora to safety.

"We have to get out of here. We're sitting ducks!" Kasia said.

"We can't run until we know where the sniper

is," Joe said. "Otherwise we could head directly towards the danger."

Jeff stretched out a hand to them and moaned, "*Help me ... please.*"

Pandora looked to Troy. "Save him!"

Troy hesitated. He shouldn't leave Pandora's side, not during an attack. But the pleading look in her eyes made him want to help. He rose to his feet.

"No!" Kasia said, and she grabbed Troy's arm. "The sniper's using him as bait to draw us out."

"I know," Troy said, "but at least I'm bulletproof."

Kasia didn't let go of his arm. "Pandora is your Principal, not Jeff."

"But we can't leave him to die," Troy argued.

But Kasia was firm. "Our only priority is Pandora's life," she said. "I'm team leader. Do as I say."

Another shot rang out and Jeff yelled in pain as a bullet blasted his leg.

"The sniper's *killing* him!" said Troy.

"Quiet!" Azumi snapped. She had her fingers on her temples as she focused hard. "Too many noises masking the gunshot ... but I think the sniper is somewhere high up ... in the direction of the bumper cars."

"Nice work, Bullet Ears!" Lennox said, and he peeked round the edge of the stall. "I can see the big wheel ... the helter-skelter ... and the house of horror."

"I'll need another shot or two to confirm," Azumi said.

"Jeff won't survive another shot!" said Troy.

Before Kasia could stop him, he sprinted out into no-man's-land and dived on top of the boy.

A bullet struck Troy in the back. The impact felt like a battering ram. Troy groaned. He might be bulletproof, but every shot still hurt like hell.

From the cover of the shooting gallery,

Lennox gave him a thumbs-up. "Good work getting the sniper to fire again!" he said with a grin. "Azumi's confirmed the location. It's the top of the helter-skelter."

Troy played dead, but he was able to look in the direction of the helter-skelter. A boy with spiked black hair came scooting down the slide. He was met at the bottom by a girl wearing a summer dress and white gloves. They seemed to have no idea of the danger they were in as they picked up the boy's backpack.

"RUN!" Troy shouted. He no longer cared if the sniper shot him again.

They both looked at him and surprise registered on their faces.

"GET OUT OF HERE! SNIPER!"

The girl grabbed the boy's hand and ran, disappearing among the panicked crowd.

"We're leaving, Troy," Kasia called. "Now!"

"Wait!" Troy cried. They knew where the sniper was located, but Troy realised they were still pinned down. The helter-skelter was in the middle of the funfair with 360 degree views. The sniper would have a clear shot whatever direction they ran.

Troy spotted a canister strapped to the dead bodyguard's utility belt. A tear gas grenade.

They couldn't see the sniper. But what if the sniper couldn't see them either?

Troy reached out and tugged the canister free, pulled the pin and dropped it in front of him. Billowing clouds of white gas filled the air. Troy spluttered and his eyes stung as he got to his feet and dragged the injured Jeff to the shooting gallery. Lennox slung the boy over his shoulder. Together they fled the funfair, the smoke screen covering their escape.

21. UNBROKEN SHIELD

Medusa strode into the briefing room, a scowl on her lean face. "The sniper got away," she said.

Troy coughed. "*How?*" His throat was still sore and his eyes red from the effects of the tear gas.

Medusa shrugged. "Your guess is as good as mine. A SWAT team rushed the helter-skelter soon after you left. But all they found was a single shell casing stuck in the floor. Forensics are trying to trace the bullet to the gun, but they're not holding out much hope for a match."

"Any news on Jeff?" Lennox asked. His T-shirt was still stained with the boy's blood.

"He's in intensive care," Medusa replied, "but

the doctors are confident he'll survive. Troy, that was a brave act of yours."

"And stupid!" Kasia muttered.

Troy frowned at her. "Why?"

"You put us all in danger ... again!" she snapped.

"No, I didn't." The first time Pandora had been the victim of an attack, he'd failed to react. This time it seemed Kasia thought he'd over-reacted.

"You disobeyed my direct command!" Kasia said.

"There was a life at stake," Troy argued.

"Yes, Pandora's! And you risked it for that slimeball Jeff."

"Without the smoke screen, we wouldn't have—"

"That's enough!" Medusa said. "Troy, Kasia's right. Pandora must *always* be your first priority. And you need to obey the team leader. Pandora's safety relies on an unbroken shield. If one part of that shield is missing, then she is vulnerable. Understood?"

Troy nodded, and the movement made him wince. He had an unusually large bruise where the sniper's bullet had hit him. And it seemed to hurt more than the other times he'd been shot. He guessed the sniper had been using an ultra high-powered rifle. In future he'd try to avoid bullets rather than catching them!

"With the sniper still at large, you'll all need to stay sharp at tomorrow night's Concert for Climate Change," Medusa went on. "The mayor is determined these attacks will not disrupt the city. He says that climate change is too important an issue to cancel the concert."

"Is Pandora still going?" Azumi asked.

Medusa nodded. "She's as stubborn as her father. Besides, all the big names will be there, including the four surviving members of the Council. Security will be tight. But this sniper seems to relish such a challenge."

22. BLACKOUT

A battalion of photographers were pointing cameras like guns at the celebrities as they arrived at the concert. Movie stars, fashion models, musicians and business gurus had all turned up to support the mayor's Concert for Climate Change. Flashes lit up the night in blinding bursts as each guest paraded along the red carpet and was interviewed by various news channels.

Troy escorted Pandora along the wide path of carpet towards the concert hall. He wore sunglasses to reduce the glare from the camera flashes. He didn't want to be blinded and fail to spot a threat in the crowd.

Azumi didn't have that problem of course. Her

blindsight allowed her to move freely without the need to see, and her talent meant her other senses were more attuned to danger. She followed behind them with an usher's badge pinned to her jacket.

Pandora stopped to answer a reporter's questions.

"After the tragic events at the funfair," the woman began, "aren't you scared to come out in public?"

"Of course I am," Pandora replied. "But I'm not going to let these terrorists win. After all, we're trying to save the planet here."

"Do you feel your father's doing enough to protect you?" the reporter asked.

Pandora nodded. "He's hired the best security for me."

"But I don't *see* any bodyguards," the reporter said with a glance around.

Troy tried not to smile as the reporter looked

right past him. With the focus on the future, young people had been invited to the concert too, so none of the bulletcatchers looked out of place on the red carpet.

"That's what makes them so effective," Pandora replied before she walked off.

As he shadowed Pandora, Troy spotted Joe on the steps to the concert hall. He was scanning the crowd, memorising faces and identifying potential suspects. Kasia and Lennox were close by, mingling with the other guests.

Over their heads was the constant buzz of drones.

Troy glanced up. He hadn't forgotten his lesson from the Reactor Room – don't just search for the obvious threat and always look up. The drone squad criss-crossed the sky like hawks, their cameras spying on everyone and everything. Guards were stationed on all the rooftops. Police had searched the

surrounding buildings. And massive floodlights lit up the city square. Every eye and ear of the Council Security Force was focused on the area of the concert hall.

There was no way on earth a sniper could get close without being detected. Now they had been given the all-clear by security, the four surviving councillors arrived in limos with their families and made their way up the red carpet to join Mayor Lomez at the entrance to the concert hall.

"Azumi, any visions?" Kasia asked over their earpieces.

"Negative," Azumi replied. "But it's odd. It's all dark."

Pandora stopped for a row of photographers desperate to get a picture of her in the stunning red dress she wore. Troy was taken aback by how similar it was to the one her avatar had worn in the Reactor Room simulation. A shudder of unease ran down his spine as he recalled how *that* scenario had ended.

As they climbed the steps with the other guests, the spotlights on the concert hall went out. A moment later the street lamps died. Then the floodlights short-circuited in a dramatic burst of sparks.

A blackout engulfed the city for several blocks.

A murmur of surprise rippled through the crowd. The square was pitch-black.

"Pandora, are you still with me?" Troy asked, reaching out for her.

"Yes," she replied.

Then someone cried out in pain.

A camera flash went off. Then another. The strobe effect of the multiple flashes that followed was eerie. As if in slow motion, Troy watched one of the councillors tumble down the steps. Blood splattered across his white tuxedo.

His wife screamed. Then a second councillor

fell. Shot through the heart. A bloody hole in her evening gown. The moment caught in a brief white flash.

The darkness returned and Kasia's voice barked in Troy's earpiece – "Protect Pandora!"

23. BLOOD

Like everyone else Troy was blind in the blackout. But his hand found Pandora's arm and he wrapped himself around her. So did Kasia and Lennox. They rallied to Troy's cry to form a body-shield for the mayor's daughter.

Azumi gripped Troy's arm. "Follow me," she said.

Azumi was not affected by the blackout, of course, and she led them between the huddles of terrified guests, up the steps and towards the safety of the foyer of the concert hall.

As she guided them through the mayhem, someone yelled in pain and they heard the *thump* of another body slumping to the ground.

Troy realised the sniper could be anywhere in the darkness. Among the photographers. In a nearby building. Even ten blocks away! All the sniper needed was an infra-red night-scope to pick off his targets one by one.

Suddenly a bullet hammered Troy in the side. He stumbled under the impact, tripping up the others. Pandora let out a cry as the four of them hit the pavement. A bullet pinged off the ground, centimetres from Troy's head.

"Keep moving!" Azumi urged. She dragged Troy to his knees. "You OK?"

"I'll live," Troy groaned as he fumbled in the dark to find Pandora again.

Emergency lighting blinked on around the square as the generators kicked in. The scene was one of sheer chaos and panic. The people in the crowd were either fleeing or cowering from the unseen shooter. Two of the councillors had been shot dead. A third was dying and the fourth seriously injured. Mayor Lomez was safely buried beneath a squad of his own bodyguards ... but his daughter lay beside Troy in a pool of blood.

"No!" Troy cried. He frantically looked for her wound.

"I thought *you* were bulletproof," Pandora said. She pointed at a red stain on Troy's shirt.

"I am," Troy replied, ignoring the pain in his side. "It's your blood."

Pandora checked herself. "But I haven't been shot."

That's when Troy saw Kasia ... lying on the ground, not moving.

24. FACE I.D.

Lennox gently shook her arm. "Kasia?"

Kasia rolled onto her back. Blood flowed from a small round hole in her chest. She might have the reflex talent, but if she couldn't see the bullet coming, then she couldn't avoid it.

Troy put his hands to the wound and applied steady pressure to stem the bleeding.

Kasia groaned and her eyes flickered open. "Pandora's ... priority," she gasped, and a trickle of blood oozed from her mouth.

"Pandora's fine, but we need to get you to a hospital," Troy told her.

"I'm ... team leader ... do as I say."

Troy ignored her. He and Kasia might have their

differences but he wasn't going to let the sniper use her as bait. He kept his hands over the wound as Joe ran over and assessed her condition.

"Bullet wound. Lower chest. High likelihood of critical internal injuries and organ trauma. Chance of survival ... less than 15%."

"Then there's a chance," Troy replied.

"Pandora's survival is at 50% but dropping the longer we stay in the open," Joe went on.

"Kasia's orders – we evac Pandora *now*," Azumi stated as she helped the mayor's daughter to her feet.

"I'm second-in-command," Troy reminded them as Kasia passed out with pain. "So I make the decisions now. We're *not* leaving her."

"We don't have time to argue," Lennox grunted as he lifted the lifeless Kasia onto his back. "Let's go."

The four bulletcatchers ran in a "closed box" around Pandora. They crossed the concert hall's plaza and crashed through the doors into the foyer. Once they were inside, they took shelter behind a pillar. Lennox laid Kasia on the carpet and reapplied pressure to her wound. Azumi and Troy kept guard over Pandora, while Joe called for emergency back-up.

"Extraction vehicle three minutes out," Medusa replied from HQ into their earpieces. "Stay put until arrival."

Troy peered out of the foyer's doors. "Any idea where the sniper is?" he asked Azumi.

She shook her head. "I couldn't pinpoint the gunshots with all the noise."

"I did," Joe said. "During the blackout there was a muzzle flash from the hotel opposite."

Troy looked across the square. The high-rise luxury hotel must have had over 500 rooms. There was no way of telling which one held the sniper. "But which room?" he asked.

"With any luck, the next shot will give his exact location away," Azumi said.

As they waited for the sniper to strike, Troy spotted a boy leaving the hotel entrance.

"Joe!" Troy said. "I need a Face I.D. Haven't we seen that boy with the skater backpack before?"

With his photographic memory, Joe only needed a single glance. "Affirmative," he said. "He was at the funfair."

25. SUBWAY

The presence of the spiky-haired boy from the helter-skelter was too much of a coincidence for Troy. He had to be connected with the sniper somehow – a spotter or a flanker to the shooter himself. Troy rose to his feet.

"Where are you going?" Joe asked.

"*When the battle is over, keep one hand on your sword*," Troy replied. "This battle isn't over – and it won't be unless we catch that sniper."

"Medusa told us to stay put," Azumi said.

"But this might be our only chance to—"

"We're losing Kasia!" Lennox interrupted. His hands were soaked with her blood.

"Where's the extraction team?" Troy cried in frustration and horror.

"One minute," came Medusa's reply. "Trauma kit in back seat."

Two blacked-out bulletproof SUVs screeched round the corner and across the square. Paying no heed to pedestrians, they mounted the kerb and drove up the ramp to the concert hall's front plaza. The first one picked up Mayor Lomez and roared away. The second waited for Pandora.

Troy and Azumi kicked open the foyer doors and bundled Pandora into the back seat. Lennox followed with Kasia in his arms. Joe jumped in and set to work right away with the trauma kit.

"Come on, Troy!" Azumi said as she climbed into the front passenger seat.

Troy shook his head. "I'm going after the boy. He could lead us to the sniper."

"*Don't* break up the shield," Azumi warned.

"We won't need a shield if the terrorists are captured," Troy argued.

"I've a bad vision about this," she said. "Troy, stay!"

Troy ignored her warning and turned to Pandora. "I have to do this … for you and Kasia."

"I know," Pandora said, taking hold of his hand. "Just don't get yourself killed."

"No chance of that," he replied with a strained smile. "I'm bulletproof, remember!"

Troy closed the door and the SUV shot away with a squeal of tyres. His last glimpse of Kasia was her deathly pale face. Joe was inserting a blood pack into her arm as Lennox gave her CPR. Troy prayed to God she'd survive.

As the SUV disappeared down the road, Troy raced off in the opposite direction. He'd seen the boy head south down Main Street. Troy weaved in between the crowds of people, press and police. As he ran, his side throbbed from the impact of the sniper's bullet. It felt like he had a cracked rib.

The crowd thinned the further Troy got from the main square and he increased his pace. Ahead he spotted a boy with a backpack turn into a side street. Troy sprinted after him. Apollo's fitness regime gave him the burst of speed he needed to catch up. Troy rounded the corner and thought for a moment he'd lost the boy. The street was deserted. Then he caught a glimpse of black spiky hair disappearing down a subway entrance.

Troy dashed across the street and down the steps. According to the sign across the entrance, the station was closed for repair. But the gate itself was unlocked. Troy slipped inside and entered the ticket hall. Only emergency lighting lit the space, giving the subway a creepy atmosphere.

The boy was nowhere to be seen. But Troy

heard footsteps echoing down the static escalator. He followed the sounds. At the bottom, Troy stepped onto a deserted platform. He looked around and listened for any sign of the boy.

In the gloom, Troy heard the unmistakable click of a rifle being chambered.

26. SHOCK TO THE SYSTEM

Only now did Troy realise how foolish he had been. The boy had led him to the sniper. But also into a trap …

Troy turned to confront his fate. The slim black barrel of a collapsible stealth rifle was aimed at his chest. But Troy was more shocked by who was holding the deadly weapon.

"*You're* the sniper?" he said in disbelief.

The spiky-haired boy smirked. Close up, his eyes were coal-black and oddly large. "And you're hard to kill," he said. "I've shot you twice. But this time you'll stay dead."

Troy held up his hands.

"Too late to surrender," the boy sniper said, and his finger curled around the trigger.

Before the boy could fire, Troy grabbed the rifle's barrel in one hand and deflected the line of fire away from himself. A bullet bounced off the subway walls. Then Troy stepped forward and palm-struck the boy in the nose. Stunned, the boy put up little resistance as Troy twisted the rifle out of his grip. Troy then swung the gun butt around and caught the boy hard in the jaw.

A perfect weapon disarm.

Action beats reaction every time, Troy thought as the boy dropped to the floor.

He shouldered the rifle, reloaded, then aimed it at the dazed sniper.

"You're coming with me," he said, and he waved the barrel in the direction of the stairs.

"Am I?" the boy replied. A look of defiance sparked in his round black eyes.

The lights overhead flickered. All of a sudden Troy felt as if he'd been struck by a bolt of

lightning. His muscles locked out, his body jerked uncontrollably and he collapsed.

The boy stood up, rubbed his bruised jaw and calmly retrieved his rifle.

"Nobody touches *my* gun," he said, and spat onto Troy's face.

Troy lay helpless on the cold hard floor, his muscles twitching. The shock to his system had paralysed him. "What ... have you done to me?" he gasped.

"Me? Nothing," the boy replied with a grin. "That's all my sister's handiwork."

A girl stepped out from the shadows. She had black hair, deep purple at the tips. Troy recognised her as the girl with white gloves from the funfair.

"You don't believe bulletcatchers are the only talented ones round here, do you, Troy?" she said as she strode over to him. She wore studded leather ankle boots and a matching black leather jacket.

"Who are you?" Troy said as the pain in his muscles slowly eased.

"Well, you've met my brother Eagle Eye," she said. "With vision eight times stronger than any human, he can spot a target over two miles away – and he never misses."

She held up a bare hand and wiggled her slim fingers. Blue sparks crackled between them. "My name's Tricity."

Troy's eyes widened in fear. "Electricity! *That's* your talent?"

Tricity nodded. "Like an electric eel. I can generate, store and channel high-voltage strikes to knock out my prey ... or to kill them."

Troy felt the hairs on the back of his neck rise. The air around him grew super-charged. "*You're* the terrorists attacking our city?"

Tricity frowned. "I'm a fighter for the Army of Freedom, if that's what you mean."

"B ... But you're my age. You can't be terrorists."

"Why not? You're a bulletcatcher," she replied. "S.P.E.A.R. have got you risking your life for spoilt rich kids. We're fighting for a far better cause. Freedom."

"But you're killing innocent people!" Troy argued. His strength was returning now.

"No one's innocent in this city," Tricity sneered. "They're all sinners. And in a war for freedom, sacrifices must be made."

Troy felt his jaw tighten in rage. That was the exact same phrase the terrorist who'd murdered his parents had used to justify his actions.

"I blacked out the city square," Tricity said with a smug smile. "That's a lot of juice for me to absorb in one go. And I need to offload some of it ..."

She reached out her hand towards Troy's heart. The air crackled and hissed with sparks.

"You may be bulletproof, Troy," she said, grinning, "but you're not shock-proof!"

27. THE VERDICT

"STOP!" A rasping voice echoed through the subway.

Tricity scowled but lowered her hand at the order. Out of a dark tunnel a black and white mask floated towards them. Then a tall man in a long black robe appeared and mounted the platform.

"I am judge, jury and executioner," he said. "Only I can decide his fate."

Tricity stepped back with a bow as The Judge strode over to them. He gazed down at Troy with his awful smiling-teardrop mask. A chill shuddered along Troy's spine. It was as if he had come face-to-face with the devil.

"Are you a sinner, Troy?" The Judge asked. "Or do you believe?"

"I ... I believe in good," Troy replied.

"And are you on the side of good?"

"Yes."

The Judge gave a cold laugh. "Then you are misled."

"No, *you* are the one who's deluded!" Troy shot back.

"Am I?" The Judge snapped. "I thought you were bulletproof."

"I am," Troy replied.

"Then why are you bleeding?" He pointed to Troy's side.

Troy looked down to where Eagle Eye's bullet had struck him. His shirt was sticky with fresh blood. Troy peeled back the material to see the bullet lodged in his side! It hadn't fully penetrated his body, but it had broken the skin. That at least explained the pain. But it didn't explain how such a thing could have happened.

Troy winced as The Judge prised the bullet from his flesh.

"It seems Medusa isn't telling you the whole truth," The Judge said, and he held the blood-stained bullet in front of Troy's eyes. "You now know my Army of Freedom have their own unique talents. But, by the looks of it, yours are fading."

All of a sudden Troy felt very vulnerable.

The Janus mask leaned in closer. "You should question who you are protecting and why," The Judge said.

"I *know* who I am protecting," said Troy.

"Do you?"

"Well, at least they're not hiding behind a mask like you!" Troy spat. "They're not the ones killing and spreading hate!"

"The Council is corrupt," The Judge said. "They and their families deserve to die."

"And what about people like my parents?" Troy

cried, his hands clenched in fury. "Those people who've done nothing wrong?"

"Sacrifices for the greater good."

"And who judges *your* actions, Judge?" Troy demanded.

The terrorist leader looked upwards. "God will judge me. My mission is to rid this city of sin. And I will. With the Council all but gone, I only need to purge the mayor and his daughter."

"I'll never let that happen!" Troy said, rising to his feet. But before he could lash out at The Judge, he was stunned by a jolt of electricity.

As Troy quivered on the floor, Tricity asked, "What's your verdict, Judge? He's seen our faces. Knows who we are."

"You make a strong case," The Judge said. He raised a fist, with his thumb sticking out to the side. "My verdict is ..."

His thumb hovered.

Troy knew that whatever direction it went in would seal his fate.

The Judge turned his thumb down.

With a devilish grin, Tricity thrust her open palm towards Troy's heart. A bolt of electricity burst out and Troy screamed as white-hot pain ripped through him.

28. DOUBT

Troy struggled to open his eyes against the blinding light. But when he did, he discovered Medusa standing by his bed in S.P.E.A.R.'s medical unit.

"How are you feeling?" she asked, dimming the glaring lights.

"Errr ... like I've been fried alive!" Troy mumbled. His mouth was dry and tasted of battery acid. A faint smell of burnt hair lingered in the air.

He sat up in bed, every muscle in his body tingling and sore. Lennox, Joe and Azumi greeted him with relieved smiles. "Where's Kasia?" he croaked.

His friends' smiles dropped and they exchanged sorrowful looks.

"Still in intensive care," Azumi replied. "Apollo has had to sedate her."

Troy closed his eyes again and tried to stop the tears that threatened to come.

"We found you on the street. Passed out," Medusa said. "What happened?"

Memories burst like exploding lightbulbs in Troy's head. He sat bolt upright. "The terrorists know about S.P.E.A.R.!" he exclaimed. "They know we have talents! And they have talents too!"

Troy told them about his encounter with Eagle Eye and the boy's ultra-vision. Then about Tricity and her ability to conduct electricity.

Medusa's eyes widened in shock. "That's beyond any power I've heard of. This changes everything."

"Where's Pandora?" Troy demanded. He tried to swing his legs out of bed but he had no strength. "The Judge has vowed to kill her and her father."

"Don't worry, she's at home," Medusa told

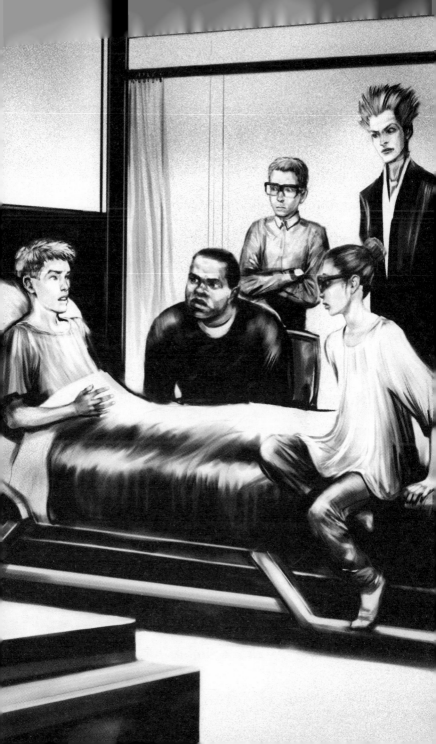

him. She eased him back down on the pillow. "Their mansion is the most secure facility in all of Terminus City."

"Nowhere's safe," Troy said. "Not with the talents on the terrorists' side."

"Pandora will be safe as long as she has you as her bulletcatcher," Medusa assured him. "We'll get you back on duty as soon as you're fit. In the meantime, the rest of the team will provide round-the-clock protection."

Troy reluctantly gave in to her command. He was in no fit state to protect anyone.

Medusa and the others left him to recover. He lay immobile and stared at the ceiling. He had so many questions buzzing around his head.

How had he survived Tricity's attack?

Was Medusa hiding the truth from him?

Who was he really protecting?

And was it worth risking his life for?

The Judge had sown seeds of doubt in his mind.

But there was one question above all.

Troy lifted the bedsheet and checked the wound on his side. The blood had clotted and a scab was forming.

Was he still bulletproof?

Part 3
Blowback

29. MESSENGER

Troy felt his skin frying to a crisp as blue arcs of electricity surged over him. His muscles jerked and twitched out of his control. The awful stench of his own burning hair filled his nostrils and his throat was sore from screaming.

Troy had never imagined he would die like this – at the hands of a teenage girl with a talent to conduct electricity at will. Bolts of lightning sparked from her fingertips and curled their jagged tendrils around Troy's helpless body as he flailed on the concrete floor of the subway platform.

"*Stop!*" Troy begged. "*Please stop!*"

To his surprise, she did. The killer current died as she dropped her hands. Troy groaned in relief and trembled as he lay on the dark platform. The girl stared at him with the cold interest of a snake eyeing its prey.

"Does it hurt?" she asked.

All Troy could do was give a feeble nod.

"Good," she said. Her pale face contorted in glee and her fingers crackled as she shot another flash of super-charged energy from her palms.

Troy was powerless to stop the attack. His own talent made him bulletproof, but he had no defence against a high-voltage shock. As the deadly electricity flooded through him, he screamed in agony. The pain ripped him apart from the inside, darkness filled his vision and his body fell limp.

"That's enough, Tricity!" The Judge ordered.

"But he isn't dead yet," Tricity said. She lowered her glowing white-hot hands. The purple tips of her jet-black hair still stood on end with static.

Troy drifted on the edge of passing out. He was

all but dead as The Judge's black and white mask floated like a ghost before his eyes. With its smile and its tears, the Janus mask seemed to mock Troy's fate.

"We *don't* want to kill him," The Judge said.

To Troy, his gruff voice seemed to come from far away, like an echo in a cave.

Beside The Judge stood a boy with spiky hair and large coal-black eyes. He was Eagle Eye, the terrorist super-sniper Troy had followed into the subway. "Why shouldn't we kill him?" Eagle Eye asked.

"This bulletcatcher can be of use to us," The Judge explained. "He can be our messenger."

"Our messenger for what?" Tricity asked.

Troy *had* to hear their plan. He fought the pain, determined not to black out.

"Our divine mission is to purify Terminus City of the Council and all sinners," The Judge said. "Tricity, before you began this bulletcatcher's execution, I told him that we intend to kill Mayor Lomez and his daughter Pandora next."

"But aren't we—?" Eagle Eye began.

"Don't dare interrupt me!" The Judge back-handed him hard across the cheek.

Eagle Eye winced then bowed his head in apology.

The Judge carried on as if he'd done nothing to the boy. "When our messenger tells S.P.E.A.R. of our plan, Medusa will send the bulletcatchers and the rest of her security force to the mayor's mansion. Once they are there, we can exterminate them all in one go."

The Judge looked up and clasped his hands together in prayer.

"And then our work will be done."

30. ALL GONE

Troy jerked awake. He was soaked in sweat and panting hard. As he sat up in the narrow bed of the medical ward, Troy saw that the underground HQ of S.P.E.A.R. – the secret close protection agency he worked for – was in darkness. There was only a soft green glow coming from the lights set into the floor. The ward was silent as death too. Just his heart-rate monitor beeping like an over-active video game.

Troy tried to calm himself.

But it had been no nightmare. What he was remembering was real.

Electrical burns still criss-crossed his body like the strikes of a whip and he felt as weak as a drained battery. But the horrific memory at least explained how he'd survived Tricity's attack. The Judge had *allowed* him to live.

Troy had been spared in order to deliver a message. One that put Pandora, her father and the entire bulletcatcher team in grave danger.

It was a trap – and Troy was responsible for setting the trap.

He had to warn his friends.

Troy ripped the monitor pad off his chest, rolled out of bed and fell to the floor with a crash. His legs were too weak to stand. So he used the wall for support as he pulled himself to his feet and stumbled out of the ward. He staggered down the corridor into the huge round chamber of S.P.E.A.R.'s briefing room. The seats were all empty and the hologram desk at the centre was switched off.

"Medusa!" he called out into the gloom. "Lennox! Joe! Azumi!"

No one answered. Just the lonely echo of his own voice.

Troy worked his way around the upper gallery. The dining area was deserted. The Rec Room was locked. He checked each dorm room, but none of the beds had been slept in.

Troy headed for the gym. Their combat and fitness instructor Apollo often trained late. Troy thumbed the keypad and the door slid open. A robed figure stood in the darkness like a pale ghost.

Troy let out a startled cry before he realised who it was ... he hardly recognised himself in the mirror wall. In a white medical gown, his body looked skeletal and frail. His sandy hair was burned black at the tips, his face was thin and dark rings shadowed his eyes like bruises. It looked as if Tricity had shocked the life out of him.

Troy let the door slide shut and stumbled to the Reactor Room. But that was deserted too. As

The Judge had predicted, the whole team must have gone to protect Pandora and Mayor Lomez from the terrorists.

Troy wiped the sweat from his brow and crossed the chamber to the Comms Room, where he collapsed into the control chair. He powered up the comms unit and pressed the talk button.

"Control to Medusa," he gasped into the mic. "Urgent message. Respond." He listened. But he got no answer from the speaker. Troy repeated his call. "Control to Medusa. Respond."

Still nothing. His fist closed around the mic as his panic grew.

"Joe! ... Azumi! ... Anyone?"

Nothing but the crackle of static ...

31. BATTLE BOOSTER

Troy pulled off his medical gown and threw it on the floor of the ward. He grabbed the fresh clothes that had been left in a neat pile on the table by his bed. Somehow he had to get to the mayor's mansion.

As he fumbled to put on his T-shirt, a dull throb in his side reminded him of the sniper bullet. Troy inspected the large purple bruise and scabbed wound on his lower ribs. He was supposed to be bullet*proof*. That was why S.P.E.A.R. had recruited him in the first place. But somehow the sniper's bullet had pierced his skin. It had stopped short of entering his body, but the wound raised alarming questions in his mind.

Had there been something special about the bullet itself? Or was his talent fading?

Troy swallowed hard, unnerved at the idea. He pulled down his T-shirt to cover the wound. Out of sight, out of mind. But still The Judge's words filled him with doubts. Was Medusa telling him the whole truth about his talent?

Troy pushed the question to the back of his mind. There were more urgent matters to deal with first. He still felt weak as he slipped on his shoes and jacket and stumbled out of the room. As he shuffled along to the ward exit, he heard the soft wheeze of a ventilator. Troy stopped and peered into the intensive care unit. There he saw a girl lying still and silent. Her skin was white as snow. Her hair platinum blonde. And the ice-blue eyes Troy knew so well were closed.

Kasia.

She was strapped to the bench of a Healer Machine, with a mask over her mouth. A sensor scanned her vital signs as a bio-laser tended to the gunshot wound to her chest.

Troy entered the room and laid a hand on her arm. Kasia's skin was cool to the touch. *Cold as a corpse*, Troy thought, and his throat tightened.

Kasia's talent was reflex. She could react six times faster than any other human. But even she'd had no chance against a bullet she couldn't see. Eagle Eye had shot her in a blackout at the star-studded Concert for Climate Change two days ago. At the time, Kasia had saved Pandora from the sniper's bullets, but now her own life hung in the balance.

Tears stung Troy's eyes and he bowed his head. The two of them hadn't always got on, but the thought that Kasia didn't know ... might never know ... how much he admired and liked her was too much to bear.

"She's stable," a soft voice said behind him.

Troy spun around. He was so used to hearing Apollo bellow combat instructions at him that he almost didn't recognise his voice when it was low and quiet. But the man's massive bulk was unmistakable. His shoulders barely fitted through the door leading from the inner office of the medical unit.

"What are you doing up?" Apollo asked. He gave Troy a sharp look.

"Medusa and the team are in serious danger and it's all my fault," Troy replied. Then he told Apollo what he'd remembered. "I tried to contact them," he finished, "but I got no response."

"That's because they've gone 'dark' to stop the Army of Freedom hacking into their comms," Apollo explained.

"But The Judge is planning an all-out attack," Troy said. "They won't be ready for it."

"Azumi will sense it coming," Apollo said with a confidence that took Troy by surprise.

"But even with her blindsight talent she might not see the danger soon enough," Troy argued. "I have to warn them."

Troy lurched for the door, stumbled and knocked over a trolley of medical supplies.

Apollo grabbed his arm and pulled him back to his feet. "You're in no fit state to go anywhere."

"Then *you* go," Troy begged.

"No can do," Apollo said with a firm shake of his bald head. "Someone has to keep HQ secure and monitor Kasia's condition. Listen, Medusa has an emergency communicator. If there's a serious problem, she'll let me know."

"What if she *can't* let you know?" Troy insisted. "I've seen what these terrorists are capable of. You haven't. They have stronger talents than us."

"Medusa is more than capable of handling anything they throw at her," Apollo said. His hand still gripped tight onto Troy's arm. "Plus, she has S.P.E.A.R.'s entire security force at the mansion. It's the terrorists who should be worried."

"You're wrong," Troy almost shouted in

frustration. "I'm going whether you like it or not." Somehow he shook himself free of Apollo's grip and headed for the door again.

"WAIT!" Apollo barked.

"You can't stop me," Troy said. He tried to sound strong, but he knew Apollo could stop him no problem.

"You are one stubborn recruit," Apollo snarled. His lip curled as he glared at Troy. Then he stepped over to a cabinet on the wall, unlocked it and removed a bottle from a glass shelf inside. He strode over to Troy.

Troy recoiled.

"In your condition," Apollo growled, "you'll need these to stand any chance against those terrorists."

Apollo twisted open the cap and shook two blue pills into Troy's hand.

"What are they?" Troy asked.

"Battle boosters," Apollo replied. "Well, that's

what we called them in the elite forces. The military designed them to help wounded soldiers survive a firefight. The pills block pain, prevent blood loss and power your body."

"Really?" Troy stared at the two pills. "They do all that?"

Apollo grinned. "They sure do. They make you super-charged. You'll feel like you can bust down walls, walk through fire and sprint like the wind. Well, at least for a few hours, and depending on how badly you've been hurt."

Troy grinned back at Apollo. "Here goes nothing," he said, and he swallowed the two pills in a flash. He took one last look at Kasia then headed for the door.

32. FORTRESS

Troy took one of S.P.E.A.R.'s high-speed auto-drives to the mansion. When he got there, he was relieved to find security in full force with armed guards patrolling the outer wall. As he approached the main gate, one of the guards blocked his path and ordered him to halt.

"I.D.," the guard demanded as three others aimed a lethal array of guns at Troy's head.

Troy took out his hologram pass and his I.D. was cleared. Two security hulks escorted him into the mansion.

"Troy!" Pandora cried as he entered the games room. "Oh Troy – you're OK!"

She almost knocked Troy over as she flung her arms around him. Her long black hair brushed

against his cheek and for a moment Troy forgot all about the danger they were in. As a S.P.E.A.R. recruit, Troy's task was to protect her – but Pandora was a girl like no other and he'd found himself falling in love with her. Not that he expected the glamorous daughter of the mayor to return his feelings.

"I heard you'd been … *electrocuted*?" she said, staring at the red lines that criss-crossed his neck.

Troy nodded. "Subways can be dangerous places," he joked. He didn't want to alarm Pandora with the news that the terrorists had talents of their own.

"Good to see you on your feet," Lennox said. The brawny bulletcatcher strode over and patted Troy on the back. Usually Troy was left reeling by one of his friend's back slaps. Lennox's Hercules gene made him 50% stronger than even the strongest weightlifter. But this time he hardly felt the impact. Apollo was right about those battle boosters!

"Shouldn't you be resting up?" Azumi said. She

turned to face Troy from behind the sunglasses that covered her blind, milk-white eyes. She was sitting with Joe, who was playing a game of hologram chess against himself.

"I thought you might be missing me," Troy told her. He joined them both by the window. When he looked out, he spotted ranks of security guards patrolling the grounds.

Lennox laughed. "No chance of that! Not with a private cinema, laser bowling alley and Prism Table. This mansion's got *everything!*"

He swept an arm round to take in the mass of high-tech kit that filled the room.

"Your focus should be on Pandora, not games!" Troy snapped.

Lennox blinked at Troy's sudden outburst. "Don't worry, it is. But everything's fine."

"What about you?" Troy turned to Azumi. "Haven't you had *any* visions?"

"None," she said, then she whispered, *"Are you sure you're OK?"*

"I'm fine," Troy replied. His blood buzzed as if he'd drunk a dozen high-energy drinks. "In fact, I've never felt better."

"I'm sure you haven't," said Joe. He stopped his game of chess and squinted at Troy's face from behind his square-framed glasses. "Dilated pupils, flushed skin, raised pulse rate. It's obvious you're on—"

"Where's Medusa?" Troy cut in. Joe's keen observation skills were vital on a mission, but his autism talent meant that he always told it exactly like it was. And sometimes he noticed a little too much.

"She's with my father," Pandora said.

"I have to speak with them both right now," Troy said. "It's urgent."

Pandora led him out of the room and down

a long hall lined with marble and glittering with glass chandeliers. The other bulletcatchers followed in formation. Even in the apparent safety of the mansion their orders were to keep Pandora in view at all times.

They crossed the entrance hall with its dramatic curved staircase and huge modern art paintings, then they entered a library panelled in wood. Rows of priceless leather-bound books lined the walls and above the fireplace hung a portrait of a beautiful raven-haired woman with dark hazel eyes, high cheekbones and rosebud lips. The similarity to Pandora was striking.

"My mother," Pandora said, when she noticed the direction of Troy's gaze.

Troy knew from S.P.E.A.R.'s mission file that Pandora's mother had been killed by a terrorist bomb five years ago. And the tremble of Pandora's chin told him the loss was still raw for her. Troy could understand her pain. It had been only a year since his own parents were murdered by the Army of Freedom in an attack on a shopping mall and his grief felt like a knife in his heart.

Pandora turned from the image of her mother to address the two bodyguards who stood by another door that led out of the library.

"I need to see my father," she said in a firm voice.

One of the bodyguards, a blond man with a neck of solid muscle, knocked on the door. A deep voice replied, "Enter."

Troy and the others followed Pandora into a drawing room. Mayor Lomez and Medusa were sitting in leather chairs looking out over the garden. The mayor was sipping from a brandy glass.

"*Hola, mi niña bonita,*" he said as he greeted his daughter with a warm smile. "What do you want, my darling?"

Troy stepped forward before Pandora had a chance to reply. "Mayor Lomez, we're all in great danger," he said. "We have to leave right now—"

"Troy, what the hell are you doing here?" Medusa demanded. Her stone-grey eyes blazed as she stood up in anger. "I'm so sorry, Carlos, for the interruption but Troy is recovering from a serious injury and it seems he's in shock."

As Medusa began to usher Troy out of the room, she hissed at him. "You don't just barge into the mayor's mansion and alarm him like this."

"You have to listen to me," Troy insisted. "The Judge has used me to set up a trap."

Medusa came to a sharp stop at the door. "What?"

Troy told Medusa of The Judge's devious plan and her spiked white hair seemed to bristle in horror. She turned back to the mayor. "We must re-assess your security. If what Troy has told me is true, then you're not safe, even here."

Mayor Lomez waved away her concern. "We don't have to worry about the Army of Freedom here," he said, and he took another sip of his brandy. "Or The Judge ..."

He rose from his chair and waved them over to stand with him by the huge bay window. Outside, a sun terrace led to an oval swimming pool that reflected the cloudless blue sky like a mirror. Beyond the pool, immaculate gardens stretched into the distance, dotted with statues, fountains and tall trees. The huge grounds all ended in a high stone wall.

"As you well know, Medusa, the outer walls here are a metre thick and bomb-proof," the mayor said. "They're topped by an electric fence. Armed guards patrol the perimeter. CCTV cameras cover every inch of the grounds and guards are stationed in the garden. We have pressure sensors embedded in the grass to alert us to intruders. The doors are fitted with electronic keypads, locks and alarms. And the windows are made of the strongest ballistic glass. So." He smiled. "I don't think we need to worry. This mansion is more secure than any fortress."

"But it won't be enough to stop them," Troy said, thinking of the terrible powers the Army of Freedom had at its disposal.

Mayor Lomez laughed. "Not even Batman could break into this place!"

33. JUDGEMENT DAY

"It's not Batman I'm afraid of," Troy said. "It's The Judge and his two talents. We're dealing with real-life villains here, not the comic book heroes I used to read about—"

A bolt of lightning struck a tree at the far end of the garden and made the lights in the mansion flicker.

"Where did *that* come from?" Pandora said. She peered up at the cloudless sky.

Azumi's face darkened. "Step away from the window!" she shouted.

Troy didn't need Azumi's blindsight to know what was about to happen. He grabbed Pandora and dived on top of her. A second later there was a loud bang as if a rock had hit the window. A round chip

appeared on the outside of the glass – in a direct line
with the mayor's head.

"See?" Mayor Lomez said. "Bulletproof glass."
He put a finger to the window and tried to wipe the
mark away. His reaction was calm, but a throbbing
vein above his left temple gave away his unease.

"GET DOWN!" Troy cried. "It's the sniper, Eagle
Eye."

Another bullet struck the window in the exact
same spot. A crack appeared in the glass. Mayor
Lomez flinched as a third bullet hit the mark. He
backed away from the window as it began to break.

Troy heard a burst of radio chatter from
Medusa's earpiece. She frowned then whispered into
her throat mic. "Delta unit proceed to the main gate.
We need back-up."

The mayor spun round. "Problems?" he asked.

Medusa shook her head. "Nothing my security
forces can't handle."

More bolts of lightning shot up from behind the perimeter wall. The electric fence sparked along its length like a firecracker, then died.

Troy pulled Pandora to her feet. "We need to get out of here," he said. "Fast."

The mayor ran over to his desk and took out a tablet from the drawer. He tapped at the screen and a wall panel slid back to reveal a large video monitor. A grid of CCTV feeds from the mansion's cameras popped up. In all of them they could see the security forces firing upon gunmen in white masks with F4000 assault rifles.

"Army of Freedom fighters!" Lennox gasped.

It was clear from the guards' panic that they were outnumbered and losing the battle.

Joe pointed to a digital map of the mansion on the screen. A series of red dots blinked in the outer grounds.

"Pressure sensors?" he asked.

The mayor nodded. "Triggered at the south end of the garden."

Lennox looked out of the window. "I don't see anyone ... apart from two guards."

Just then one of the guards dropped to the grass. A moment later his partner flew backwards as if he'd been kicked by a horse.

Joe's brow creased. "That's very interesting," he said.

"Interesting?" Lennox cried. "Weird and scary more like!"

They all watched in horror as a security guard sprinted towards the mansion – to be stopped in her tracks when a stone statue toppled from its plinth. She was crushed beneath its weight.

Pandora clasped Troy's hand. "What's going on?" she asked, her voice shaking.

"We're under attack," said Troy, "from The Judge's talents."

The two bodyguards who'd been guarding the drawing room burst in. "The outer defences have been breached!" the blond guard cried.

Gunmen in faceless white masks began to appear along the entire length of the garden wall.

"Enact Code Red protocol," Medusa ordered. "Evacuate the mayor and his daughter. Now."

As the two bodyguards strode over to escort the mayor out, a face appeared on the video feed from the main gate. It was a chilling black and white mask.

The Judge's smiling–crying face filled the screen. Then his rasping voice spoke.

"Judgement Day, Mayor Lomez."

34. CODE RED

Troy bundled Pandora out of the drawing room. Lennox, Azumi and Joe ran alongside. In front, Medusa and the two bodyguards rushed Mayor Lomez down the hall towards the underground garage of the mansion.

Code Red protocol was S.P.E.A.R.'s emergency evacuation procedure. A bulletproof SUV was prepped at all times to speed the mayor and his daughter away to a secret safe house.

"This shouldn't be happening!" Mayor Lomez said. He sounded more angry than scared.

"I can only apologise," Medusa replied as she stopped and entered a code into a keypad. "But I promise to get you both to a safe place."

A hidden door slid open and Medusa led the

way down two flights of stairs. At the bottom they went through another security door and entered the garage. The SUV was waiting for them, doors open, driver at the wheel, engine running.

"I've a bad vision about this," Azumi hissed.

"No surprise there!" Lennox said. His tone was sarcastic as the sound of distant gunfire boomed down the stairwell.

"We don't have much choice," Medusa said. "Let's move." She pushed the mayor ahead.

After a quick look around the deserted garage, Troy led Pandora past the mayor's long line of luxury sports cars and motorbikes. As they approached the SUV, a girl with black and purple hair stepped out from behind a gold Aston Martin.

"Watch out!" Troy cried. "It's Tricity." He pushed Pandora behind a jet-black Lotus.

Bolts of white-blue light burst from Tricity's hands. The SUV lit up, its headlights exploded, its

windscreen shattered and its tyres burst into flame. The driver inside jerked and screamed. In seconds, the vehicle was a ball of fire.

"*What now?*" the mayor cried. He huddled in the shelter of a soft-top Ferrari with Medusa and the others.

"Do you have the key to any of these cars?" Joe asked.

"Upstairs in my office, with all the other keys," the mayor replied.

"That's no help to us," Joe said.

The mayor gritted his teeth and hissed at him. "You people advised me to keep them there for security reasons!"

The next target for Tricity's electrical storm was an orange Harley Davidson chopper. The bike's petrol tank ignited and an explosion rocked the garage.

"We can't stay here much longer," Medusa said as she shielded the mayor from the blast of heat.

"There's another SUV prepped in the driveway," the blond bodyguard said.

His partner, a dark-haired Hispanic woman, pulled out a snub-nosed machine gun from her jacket and fired at Tricity.

Tricity ducked behind a concrete pillar.

"GO!" the bodyguard said. "I'll cover you."

Bullets blasted the pillar as they sprinted back to the stairwell. They bounded up the stairs two at a time and dashed into the mansion's grand entrance hall. Troy spotted a black SUV parked outside as the blond bodyguard scanned the gravel driveway. "Can't see any A.F. fighters," he said.

At that moment his partner burst from the stairwell. "Hurry!" she gasped as she slammed the door behind her. "Electro-girl's trying to short-circuit the locks."

The blond bodyguard flung open the front door, checked the route was clear then waved to his partner – *Go!* Gun at the ready, the bodyguard had taken only two steps when a bullet shot her dead centre in the head. She crumpled to the ground and Pandora stifled a shocked cry with her hand.

"Eagle Eye!" Troy said. He tried to locate the sniper in the mansion grounds. "He never misses."

"It's fifty metres to the SUV," Joe said. "That's ten seconds out in the open. There's eight of us. Eagle Eye fired one round per second at the window. So none of us will survive."

"But Troy's bulletproof," Lennox pointed out

"He can't protect all of us," said Medusa.

Troy nodded in agreement. Besides, he didn't fancy running a suicide mission to the vehicle. His talent ... *if it still worked* ... would stop a bullet or two. But ten bullets would push him beyond his limit, even pumped up on battle boosters.

Pandora's hazel eyes were wide with terror. "We're trapped then?" she said.

"Carlos, you have a safe room, don't you?" said Medusa.

The mayor nodded. "Yes, next to the master bedroom."

They turned and ran up the stairs. As they reached the landing, two gunmen in white masks kicked down the front door and fired up at them. Troy looked back and saw a short, round-faced boy behind the terrorists. His dark snake-like eyes were fixed on Troy. Bullets pinged off the marble walls and ripped across priceless artworks. All of a sudden Troy felt a tap on his arm and there was a hole in his jacket. He'd been hit. But he felt zero pain.

"This way!" Mayor Lomez cried, and he led them down a wide corridor. But before they could reach the master bedroom, the door slammed shut. Then a huge vase of flowers flew off a table and smashed the blond bodyguard over the head. He reeled from the blow.

"The door won't open." Medusa cursed as she yanked on the handle.

Lennox gave it a go. But he only succeeded in ripping the handle off.

"They're coming!" Azumi cried.

Lennox threw his body against the door again and again ... but each time he bounced off like a rubber ball. As he moved back for another try, a large mirror flew from the wall and struck him in the face. "What the hell?" he cried as blood streamed from a gash on his head.

"My room!" Pandora yelled. "We can get in that way."

They ran into her bedroom and crossed to an en-suite dressing room. Pandora put her thumb to a sensor pad and a full-length mirror slid back to reveal a steel door. The sound of pounding feet and angry shouts drew closer. The hidden door opened and they dived inside.

35. SAFE ROOM

The safe room was designed for four people – none of them the size of Lennox and the blond bodyguard – so it was a little crowded as they locked and bolted the steel door behind them. A cubicle with a toilet and a shower took up one corner. A small sink and cooking unit filled another. A narrow bunk-bed was mounted on one wall and on the opposite side were shelves of supplies and a small desk with a screen above it.

The mayor sat in the only chair and keyed a password onto the screen. Pandora perched on the lower bunk with her head in her hands. Troy put an arm around her to comfort her. Azumi found the medical box and Joe helped her to dress Lennox's injury. Medusa and the blond bodyguard stood behind the mayor as the screen blinked to life to show a grid of security cameras.

A view of the underground garage showed the SUV still in flames.

"Why hasn't the fire sprinkler system kicked in?" the bodyguard asked.

"It's been shut down," the mayor said. He pointed to a flashing icon on the security app.

"Who by?" Medusa asked.

"The Judge or Tricity," Joe replied as he tied Lennox's bandage. "Water and electricity don't mix well. The terrorists wouldn't want to electrocute themselves by mistake."

Another video feed showed the main gate where all the mayor's security guards lay dead or dying.

"I don't believe this," Mayor Lomez muttered. The vein over his left temple throbbed. "It's—"

But he fell silent as a camera in the master

bedroom showed a robed man enter and walk up to a tall mirror. Beside him stood Tricity and the snake-eyed boy Troy had spotted earlier. The figure looked up at the lens from behind his black and white mask.

"Knock, knock!" The Judge said, and he rapped on the mirror. "You can't hide from your sins, Mayor Lomez."

"I've no sins to hide," the mayor snapped into the mic on the screen. "Why are you here, Judge?"

"You know why I'm here," The Judge replied. "Unlock the door and we can discuss this like civilised men."

"Civilised?" Mayor Lomez spat. "Do you think I'm stupid?"

"No, I think you're guilty," The Judge said. "But first you must stand trial."

Mayor Lomez laughed. "You're the one who's guilty ... and insane!"

Medusa spoke into the mic. "Judge, exit this property right now or—"

"Ah, Medusa!" The Judge cut in, his tone delighted. "You and I also have matters to discuss."

Shock flickered across Medusa's pale face as she realised that The Judge knew her voice. She swallowed hard then cleared her throat. "The police are on their way," she said. "They have orders to shoot to kill."

"I don't fear the police," The Judge said. "I don't fear you, Medusa. I fear no one ... bar God. It is *you* who should tremble in fear and surrender up your souls. I have cut all comms. No one is coming to your rescue ..."

As The Judge talked on, Azumi leaned close to Troy. "How many of us made it into this room?" she whispered.

Troy frowned. "Eight."

"Then why do I sense *nine* people in here?"

Troy looked around. He counted eight. The door to the toilet cubicle was ajar, but he couldn't see anyone else.

"... Now, open up the safe room or God have mercy on your souls," said The Judge.

"No – you leave now or I'll show *you* no mercy, Judge," Mayor Lomez replied. "Your reign of terror is over."

Now it was The Judge's turn to laugh. "My work ridding Terminus City of sin has barely begun," he said. "And from where I'm standing, you're in no position to make threats."

"The steel doors have an internal locking system – even your electro-girl can't short-circuit it," the mayor said. "We're protected by a metre of reinforced concrete and we've our own air filtration system and supplies. Crawl back to your hell-hole, Judge. You won't *ever* get in."

"I wouldn't be so sure of that," The Judge said.

He raised his hands to the camera like a wizard and called out, "Open Sesame!"

Troy and the others watched in horror as the door unlocked itself from the inside.

36. THE TRIAL

"Let the trial begin," The Judge declared.

He struck the desk with a small wooden mallet and a sharp *crack* like a gunshot rang off the walls of the drawing room.

Troy's eyes darted around, looking for ways to escape or fight back. But they were surrounded on all sides. Two gunmen in white masks guarded the door. Another two stood by the bay window. Behind The Judge stood Tricity, Eagle Eye and two new talents. A girl with golden brown hair and sand-coloured skin. "Shifter," as the mayor had called her when she'd suddenly appeared by the safe-room door. She'd been the invisible *ninth* person

in the safe room – the one who had unlocked the door. Her talent was camouflage. Her skin was like a chameleon's, which explained the mystery of the two guards who had been knocked down in the garden by an unseen force.

The boy was silent and still as a cobra waiting to strike. His talent had yet to be revealed, but Troy had his suspicions.

"Will the accused step forward," The Judge said.

"This is a farce!" said Mayor Lomez. He ignored The Judge's request and the masked gunmen, and instead he strode over to the drinks cabinet and poured himself a large brandy. "You've taken your crusade too far, Judge."

Troy was stunned by the mayor's brazen nerve. Then he noticed him take a handgun from the cabinet and slip it into his belt under his jumper. His courage was inspiring. *No wonder he's the mayor of Terminus City*, Troy thought.

"Respect the court, Mayor," The Judge warned. "You are accused of deceit, fraud and murder."

Mayor Lomez downed his drink and laughed. "What sort of kangaroo court is this?" he demanded. "Those are the crimes *you're* guilty of, Judge."

"I'm not the one on trial," The Judge said. "You are."

The Judge nodded to a gunman and the mayor was forced back into line with Troy and the others.

"For those present," The Judge said, "let it be known that Mayor Lomez is the leader of the Army of Freedom. He's lied about the threat to Terminus City. He's held on to power by means of force and fear. And he is responsible for the deaths of the Council members and countless citizens—"

"These claims are outrageous," Medusa cut in. "What sort of fools do you take us f—"

"Silence, Medusa!" The Judge snapped. "Your trial is next."

Pandora stepped forward, as brave as her father. "My father would never do such things!" she yelled. "He's the elected mayor of the city. The people trust him to *destroy* the Army of Freedom, not to lead it."

"My dear girl, social control is best managed through fear," The Judge replied. "By inventing an external threat, people like your father can keep society off balance and paranoid. Dictators can then position themselves as the people's only hope. And thus they gain absolute power over them."

"Your accusations are unfounded," said Mayor Lomez. "No one will ever believe you!"

"Tricity, assist the mayor with his confession," The Judge ordered.

As Tricity pointed a sparking finger, Mayor Lomez glared at her. "Do your worst, but you won't get a word out of me," he said.

"Fine," Tricity said with a shrug. "Perhaps your daughter can persuade you to talk."

Before Troy could react, a bolt of electricity shot out and struck Pandora in the chest.

"No!" Troy cried. He dropped down with Lennox and Azumi to shield Pandora from further attack.

Tricity's hand crackled and glowed as an energy bolt charged up in her palm.

"STOP!" Mayor Lomez shouted, his face red with anger. "You're under *my* command!"

"Not any more," The Judge replied. He held up a hand for Tricity to stop. "But thank you for your confession."

Medusa, Troy and the others stared in disbelief at the mayor.

"Father?" Pandora gasped as tears of pain and shock welled up in her eyes.

"I-I-I meant I'm in charge ... I'm the mayor," he stuttered. He turned away from his daughter's gaze.

"Your immoral plan has turned in on itself," The Judge went on. "You used me as a weapon to strike fear into the citizens of this city. Now that weapon is pointing back at you. This is what spies call *blowback*."

The Judge struck his mallet on the table.

"Mayor Lomez, you're guilty as charged. I sentence you to death."

37. EXECUTION

"This can't be true," Troy said as The Judge laid a handgun on the table. "Your terrorists targeted Pandora. Why would Mayor Lomez want to kill his own daughter?"

The Judge's black and white mask turned towards Troy. "Mayor Lomez made Pandora appear to be a target, so he could create more fear among the people, demand more power from the Council and keep any suspicion away from himself. In the subway I told you to question who you protect and why. Remember? I'm just the weapon. Mayor Lomez is the one who pulls the trigger."

Troy looked to the mayor for a denial, but the truth was written all over his pale face. Troy realised that *this* was the man responsible for his parents' murder.

The Judge cocked his gun and aimed it at the mayor. "As judge, jury and executioner ..."

Mayor Lomez looked to his blond bodyguard. "For heaven's sake, protect me!"

The bodyguard shook his head and backed away.

"It seems, Mayor, that you're losing your grip on power," The Judge said. He shot the bodyguard between the eyes.

Unprotected, Mayor Lomez now seized Troy and held him in front of him as a shield. From his belt, he pulled out the hidden handgun and fired at The Judge.

The shot was at point-blank range, but the bullet simply shattered a mirror behind The Judge. Then the gun flew from the mayor's grip and ended up in the hands of the strange snake-eyed boy.

"Had you forgotten that Feng's talent is telekinesis?" The Judge said. "He can move objects with his mind."

Troy's suspicions had been right – the boy's talent explained toppling statues, closing bedroom doors and flying ornaments.

"Unfortunately, Mayor, the bulletcatcher you're holding is losing *his* talent," The Judge said with a cruel laugh. "He's no longer bulletproof."

The Judge fired.

Troy felt the bullet's impact as it passed right through his shoulder. Again there was no pain – but the mayor screamed and the two of them fell to the floor. Pandora rushed to her father's side as blood poured from a gaping wound in his chest.

"I'm sorry ... *mi niña bonita*," her father groaned. "I only wanted to keep you safe ... Terminus City safe ... After your mother's death, I vowed to take absolute control ... to stop it ever happening again ... it was a choice between safety and freedom ... can't have both ..."

Mayor Lomez's eyes glazed over. Pandora hugged her dead father's body as tears poured down her face.

Lennox tried to sit Troy up. "Troy! Are you all right?" he asked.

Troy nodded. He examined the second hole in his jacket. There was no blood, but he knew it wasn't his talent that had saved him. It was the battle boosters – and he dreaded what would happen when their powers wore off.

"You're the devil incarnate!" Medusa spat, and her stone-grey eyes burned at The Judge. "How can you justify shooting this boy to kill the mayor?"

"I'm not the one who put him in the line of fire," The Judge replied. "That was you, Medusa." He paused. "By the way, did you inform your recruits that their talents can fail? No, I didn't think so. As I told you, Troy, Medusa wasn't telling the whole truth. All she cares about is S.P.E.A.R. She doesn't care that she's risking your lives."

Troy looked to Medusa. Her grey eyes were wide and she was shaking her head. "Don't listen to him," she begged. "You know that *you* are my priority."

"And did you tell them about your *own* talent for mind control?" The Judge asked.

Troy swapped stunned looks with Lennox and the others.

"That explains a lot," Joe said, in a matter-of-fact tone.

"Her powers have become weak over time," The Judge admitted, "yet they are still strong enough to influence the thinking of a vulnerable child."

"He's lying!" Medusa cried, but Troy recalled the stone-grey eyes that had filled his vision that day in the hospital. *"Join S.P.E.A.R. It's your best hope,"* she had said, and the decision was made for him.

240

"Your trial is at an end, Medusa," The Judge said. "The verdict is in."

As he aimed his gun, Medusa snarled, "And when is your trial, Judge?"

"My time will come," he declared. "Everybody has their Judgement Day."

And he pulled the trigger.

38. BACK FROM THE DEAD

In the nano-second before The Judge's gun fired its bullets, Azumi warned Troy and the others, "Close your eyes! Cover your ears!"

A moment later the bay window exploded in a hailstorm of glass. The two terrorist guards were blown off their feet and The Judge was knocked back into his chair. His aim was thrown off and the bullet meant for Medusa's heart clipped the side of her head instead. Dazed, she dropped to her knees as blood streamed down her face. Then a stun grenade clattered across the floor. There was a lightning-white flash and a bang like a thunder clap.

Despite Azumi's warning, Troy's ears still rang.

But he wasn't stunned or blinded like The Judge and his talents. Through the smoke, Troy saw the doors to the drawing room fly open and a guardian angel appeared ...

Kasia!

In the blink of an eye, she disarmed both remaining guards then knocked them out with the butt of their guns. A moment later Apollo strode in from the shattered window carrying the largest assault rifle Troy had ever seen in his life.

"You got my message then?" Medusa groaned as Apollo lifted her up and put her back on her feet.

"Loud and clear," Apollo replied.

"Kasia, you're OK!" Troy said, standing up to greet her.

"Back from the dead." She grinned and Troy knew from the sparkle in her ice-blue eyes that she was on battle boosters too.

"Let's move!" Apollo barked as another wave of

gunmen in white masks surged across the mansion grounds towards them.

Troy dragged the sobbing Pandora off her father's dead body. "He's gone, for good," he told her, without a shred of pity for the man. "But you're not ... and I've sworn to protect you."

They dashed out onto the sun terrace after the others. Apollo's rifle thundered and masked gunmen dropped like nine-pins in a bowling alley. Those who survived Apollo's attack took cover and returned fire every bit as fierce.

"We're cut off from our escape vehicle," Kasia said as they sheltered behind the pillars by the swimming pool.

"What about the SUV out front?" Joe reminded them.

"Good thinking," said Medusa. "Apollo, cover us."

The assault rifle roared again. Joe was leading the way when his head rocked back and he spat blood. Another invisible blow doubled him over.

"It's Shifter!" Troy cried.

"Where is she? I can't see her," Lennox said. He stepped to Joe's defence and raised his beefy fists.

"Don't worry, I can sense her," Azumi said, and she launched a perfect side kick into thin air.

There was a grunt and for a brief second a pair of dark brown eyes shimmered before them … then vanished.

"You can't hide from me," Azumi said as she fought the air. Her strong legs whirled and her fists flew.

"Come on," Medusa yelled. "To the SU—"

A huge bolt of electricity blasted her backwards.

"Not so fast!" Tricity yelled as she strode out of the drawing room. A twin high-voltage beam shot from her palms. Troy shielded Pandora with his body and he got the full force of the strike. The battle boosters meant he didn't suffer the excruciating pain he had before, but he still felt each and every muscle spasm as he thrashed on the floor, unable to save himself.

Lennox rushed at Tricity. She turned on him. Lightning coursed over his body but it didn't stop him. He charged into her like a steel battering ram. She went down and they tumbled head over heels into the garden.

When Troy's muscles stopped their violent twitching, he became aware of someone shaking his arm. Pandora was staring down at him, her eyes wet with fresh tears. "Troy! Troy!"

"I'm good," he said, realising her tears were for him. He got back to his feet and scanned the battle scene.

Joe had recovered from Shifter's sneak attack and was putting his glasses back straight. Beside him Medusa's body twitched but she showed no other

signs of life. Apollo was still keeping the masked gunmen at bay. His rifle blasted away, but he was running out of bullets fast. Then the pillar he was crouched behind began to topple over.

"Apollo!" Troy shouted. "Watch out!"

Apollo rolled to one side as the stone pillar came crashing down. It shattered into a hundred pieces. Then one jagged lump lifted off the ground and flew at Kasia's head. She ducked as her reflex talent saved her from the fatal blow.

"That's Feng again," Troy cried. He pointed to the dark-haired boy standing by the broken bay window, his snake-like eyes narrowed in focus.

"You get Pandora to safety!" Kasia ordered as she dodged another chunk of stone. "We can handle these talents."

39. LINE OF FIRE

Troy rushed Pandora along the path to the far end of the mansion. The SUV was still parked in the gravel drive. He looked back. His friends were locked in battle with Tricity, Feng and Shifter. Apollo was down to his last clip of ammo. Troy wondered if he should be deserting them at all. Then a bullet pinged off the brick wall of the mansion, close to Pandora's head.

On instinct, Troy leaped into the line of fire. A second bullet bounced off the wings of a stone angel statue, a good metre from where they stood. Troy heard someone curse and Eagle Eye the sniper stepped out from behind a bush. His rifle was aimed at Pandora.

Troy was stunned. "I thought you never missed," he shouted.

"I don't!" Eagle Eye snapped, coming closer to get a better shot. The boy was blinking over and over as tears streamed from his large round eyes. Troy realised the stun grenade had done Eagle Eye more damage than anyone else.

As the sniper wiped his watery eyes, Joe ran up behind him and kicked his legs from under him. "Go!" Joe shouted to Troy as he wrestled the rifle from Eagle Eye.

Troy grabbed Pandora's hand and dashed across to the SUV. He flung open the driver's door and they jumped in ... but they couldn't start the car.

"You'll be needing this," a rasping voice said.

The masked face of The Judge leered at them from the other side of the window. He held a sleek black key fob in one hand. In the other was a gun.

"Get out!" he ordered with a wave of the gun.

Troy shielded Pandora as they stood before The Judge.

"Is she *really* worth protecting?" The Judge asked. He aimed his barrel at Troy and Pandora. "Are you ready to lay down your life for the daughter of the man responsible for your parents' murder?"

"Whatever her father did, Pandora is innocent," Troy said. "You're the one with blood on your hands."

"Pandora bears the sins of her father," The Judge spat. "She can't be allowed to live." His finger curled round the trigger. "Last chance ..."

Troy stood his ground between The Judge and Pandora.

The moment the bullet struck his chest, he shoved Pandora aside, out of the line of fire. "RUN!" he yelled.

As Troy slumped to the ground, he watched Pandora sprint up the drive. His chest burned where the bullet had hit him and he knew the battle boosters were wearing off.

The Judge stood over him as he reloaded his

gun. "A heroic sacrifice, Troy," he said, "but you've only delayed her judgement."

The Judge took slow, careful aim at Pandora as she ran and shot her in the back.

 40. DIVINE JUSTICE

"NOOOOO!" Troy screamed as Pandora stumbled then tried to stagger on a few more steps.

The Judge fired again and she fell face first into the dirt.

"YOU DEMON!" Troy bawled. "YOU FACELESS FREAK!"

"Careful what you say, Troy," The Judge said, his voice as cold as ever, "or you'll find yourself on trial again."

"Your trials aren't real trials!" Troy spat. "They're excuses for murder!"

"I am the angel of death," The Judge declared. "I've been sent to cleanse this city of sin – and so I will."

The wound in Troy's chest was agony and blood

was seeping out of the holes in his jacket. He could see his friends still bravely battling the talents. But Apollo had run out of ammo and been shot in the leg. He was trying to drag Medusa to safety. Azumi's glasses were smashed and her mouth was bleeding, and it was clear she was losing the fight with Shifter – the ghost girl only visible when Azumi landed an occasional punch or a kick. Joe was pinned to the ground by Eagle Eye, who had his rifle pressed up against Joe's throat. Lennox had Tricity in his powerful grip. Arcs of electricity flowed down his back like a cape. He was roaring in pain and rage yet somehow he was able to stand up to her attack. *But for how much longer?*

Then Troy saw Kasia sprint up the path. She weaved and dodged as bricks, stones and chunks of broken pillar flew at her. When she spotted Troy at The Judge's feet, she ground to a sudden halt beside the angel statue. Her look was one of shock and dismay. Then she turned back to the battle and shouted in fury, "Is that all you can manage, Feng? Pebbles and rocks?"

More missiles flew at her as she ran onto the drive.

Troy knew they were defeated. He glared up at the black and white mask of The Judge.

"You're no angel," he said bitterly. "You're a devil. That's why you hide behind a two-faced mask."

"I'll tell you the reason I wear this Janus mask," The Judge said. "Janus is the Roman god of all beginnings. He presides over the start and end of any conflict. The doors of his temple open in time of war and close to mark the coming of peace. Under my rule, there'll be a new beginning as I bring true peace to Terminus City."

The Judge aimed his gun at Troy's head.

"But first, I must cleanse the city of you and your bulletcatchers," he said.

Troy had no strength to fight back. As the battle boosters faded into nothing, the pain bloomed and his lifeblood flowed out.

He was no longer bulletproof, and he braced himself for the killing shot.

Then out of the sky flew an angel. It crushed The Judge and he crumpled into the gravel next to Troy. His black and white mask wept tears of blood.

41. HIDDEN TALENT

"That was close!" Kasia said as she sank to her knees beside Troy. "I almost didn't get out of the way in time."

Troy stared at the stone angel that Feng had launched at Kasia just as she crept up behind The Judge. "I guess that's what you call divine justice," he said with a grim smile.

He heard a crunch of gravel as Feng appeared. The boy froze when he saw The Judge lying dead beneath the angel. For a moment Troy thought Feng might raise it up and crush him and Kasia with it. But Feng was horrified at his fatal mistake. He backed away and shouted to the other talents, "The Judge is dead!"

Now that his master no longer held the balance of power, Feng bolted and disappeared into the trees.

"So much for The Judge's loyal followers," Kasia said. She helped Troy to sit up. His chest burned like fire and his shirt was soaked with blood.

"We need to get you to a hospital," Kasia said, and she grabbed the key fob from The Judge's limp hand.

"What about the others?" Troy wheezed.

Kasia looked over her shoulder. "They're just tidying up the mess," she said with a grin.

Azumi had leaped into the air and was in the middle of a devastating spinning kick. A second later a body shimmered into view at her feet. Her heel had caught Shifter's invisible jaw and the girl had been knocked out cold.

Lennox was lit up like a lightbulb. Streaks of electricity were raining down on him as he lifted the furious Tricity above his head. Then, with a mighty

effort, he tossed her into the swimming pool. There was a massive explosive spark followed by a hiss of steam. When the air cleared, Tricity's charred body could be seen floating in the water.

"You were right, Joe," Lennox called out. His curls of black hair were smoking. "Water and electricity don't mix!"

But Joe wasn't in such a winning position as the others. He'd managed to throw Eagle Eye off, only for the sniper to turn his rifle on him. Yet Joe appeared unfazed as Eagle Eye aimed the weapon and pulled the trigger ...

Click ... click ... click.

"You'll be needing these," Joe said. He opened his hand to reveal the bullets he'd taken from the gun during their struggle.

"Give them back!" Eagle Eye snarled.

"Of course," Joe said, and he tossed the bullets at Eagle Eye's feet.

As he scrabbled on the ground to reload, Eagle Eye never knew what hit him. Lennox strode up behind him and struck the boy on the head like a sledgehammer driving a post into the ground.

"It always amazes me," Joe said, "how easy it is to distract the eye."

Apollo, limping badly, appeared with Medusa slung over his back. "The Judge's gunmen are in retreat," he grunted as he lowered Medusa into the back seat of the SUV. "But when they realise we're out of ammo, they might return to finish us off."

Now their opponents were dispatched, Lennox, Joe and Azumi sprinted across the drive to join them in the SUV.

"Let's go," Apollo ordered, and he herded them into the vehicle.

"But what about Pandora?" said Troy. He staggered over and sank down by her lifeless body. He brushed a lock of raven hair from her angel face.

Troy loved this girl. He'd been willing to die for her. Yet that hadn't been enough.

"We're too late to save her," Apollo said, laying a hand on him, "but *you* need urgent medical attention. Come on."

"We can't give up on her."

"Troy, you took a bullet for her – several by the looks of it. No one could ask you to do more. But we have to go. Now."

Troy no longer had the strength to stand. As Apollo lifted him into his arms, Troy thought he saw Pandora's eyes flicker.

"Wait!" he said. "She's alive."

"Don't fool yourself," Apollo said as he carried Troy to the SUV. "Only a bulletcatcher like you could survive two rounds in the back."

42. FREE CHOICE

"I cut my knee open once falling off my bike. By the time I'd limped home and told my mother, it was healed. I always thought I was just lucky." Pandora laughed. "Who knew I had a talent for self-healing?"

Troy listened in amazement as he lay on the narrow bed in S.P.E.A.R.'s medical ward. A Healer Machine hummed beside him, its bio-lasers tending to his gunshot wounds.

Pandora sat next to him, holding his hand. For Troy that was the most wonderful feeling in the world. Second only to seeing Pandora come back to life and sit up on the gravel of the mansion's drive.

"So you never needed us to protect you at all!" Kasia said with a roll of her eyes. She lay in the bed next to Troy's, attached to her own Healer Machine.

"I wouldn't say that," Pandora replied, giving Troy's hand a squeeze.

"Well, who'd have thought I had a *double* talent?" Lennox said. He thrust out his broad chest. "I'm shockproof!"

"That's not technically true," Joe said as he cleaned his glasses with his T-shirt. "You just have a higher resistance due to your bulk."

Lennox frowned. "Are you saying I'm *fat*?"

"He's saying you're lucky too," Azumi said, sucking at her swollen lower lip.

Troy winced as the Healer Machine laser-stitched his skin. "Well, I wish I had a self-healing talent," he said.

"We could always take a battle booster," Kasia said with a wink.

"No more battle boosters for you two!" Apollo growled from the inner office. "Drugs are never the answer. You both need time to heal properly."

Medusa walked stiffly into the ward. Her white hair was styled in its usual spikes but now it made her appear like she was still being electrocuted.

"I've good news," she announced. "The Army of Freedom has disbanded following news of The Judge's death. His talents have vanished too. It seems The Judge ruled with an iron fist and no one has stepped forward to take his place."

"What about the Council?" Azumi asked. "Who's going to run the city now?"

"There's only one surviving Council member and she is in no fit state to rule. She's proposed that Pandora governs the city."

Pandora's mouth fell open. "Me?" she exclaimed.

Medusa nodded. "You're the people's choice. For the sake of law and order, we've not disclosed your father's links with the terrorists. And we know you had nothing to do with it."

Pandora hung her head and sighed. "My father may have been wrong in his methods, but his reasons were good."

After a minute's silence, she looked up with a steely glint in her hazel eyes. "We need to make Terminus City safe," she said. "But the price cannot be freedom. Peace in the shadow of fear is not peace. We have to have the choice to live free."

"You're going to make a fine mayor," Medusa said with a rare smile. "And S.P.E.A.R. will continue to protect you. That's if my bulletcatchers wish to stay?"

Medusa turned to Troy and the others, with a pained look on her pale face.

"I can only apologise for using my talent to influence you," she said. "There are so few of you in the world ... When I met a talent capable and worthy of being a bulletcatcher, I did anything in my power to recruit them."

Medusa bowed her head in shame, fixing her

eyes on the floor. "I'll understand if you want to leave," she said. "As Pandora said, you have the choice to live free."

Troy and the others exchanged looks but said nothing.

Then Joe spoke up. "The question is, if we had known then what we know now, would we have made a different choice?"

Troy thought back to that moment in hospital. Alone, orphaned and scared. Would he have made a different choice?

"There was never any doubt in my mind," Kasia said. "I'm still in."

"We're a team, aren't we?" Lennox grinned. "I'm staying if you're staying."

Joe nodded. "This is where I belong. My autism is my strength at S.P.E.A.R."

"And my blindsight has purpose," Azumi agreed. "Besides, I stick by my friends."

"What about you, Troy?" Kasia asked. "Without your talent, you've only got your training to rely on."

"I may not be able to catch bullets any more," Troy said, smiling at her and the rest of the team, "but I'll *always* be a bulletcatcher."

Do **YOU** have what it takes to be a bulletcatcher?

Find out with this test!

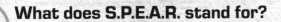

1 **What does S.P.E.A.R. stand for?**

a) Safety Protector and Enhanced Armed Recruit

b) Super Powered Entity And Raider

c) Security, Protection and Elemental Assault Response

d) Santa Promises Extra Apples and Raisins

2 **Joe's talent is …**

a) reflex

b) electricity

c) invisibility

d) recall

The tattoo on
the neck of the
terrorist is the
kanji symbol for:

a) fire

b) water

c) earth

d) wind

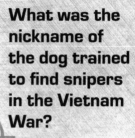

What was the
nickname of
the dog trained
to find snipers
in the Vietnam
War?

a) Eagle Eyes

b) Bullet Ears

c) Top Gun

d) Dead Shot

The three factors
that determine
your speed to an
attack situation are
reaction, response
and ...

a) readiness

b) release

c) rapidity

d) results

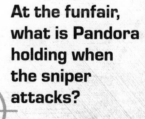

At the funfair,
what is Pandora
holding when
the sniper
attacks?

a) candy floss

b) rifle

c) popcorn

d) teddy bear

7 Who are the A.F.?

a) the Army of Fighters

b) the Army of Freedom

c) the Armed Front

d) the Attack Force

8 The battle booster pills are what colour?

a) red

b) green

c) yellow

d) blue

9 What vehicle do Troy and Pandora hide behind in the garage?

a) a jet-black Lotus

b) a gold Aston Martin

c) a silver SUV

d) a soft-top Ferrari

10 Who opens the door to the safe room?

a) Tricity

b) Eagle Eye

c) Shifter

d) Feng

 # Results

0-2: YOU NEED PROTECTION!

Hire yourself a bulletcatcher quick! Or read *S.P.E.A.R.* again to get the answers to protect yourself. Troy didn't know anything about close protection at first, so there's still hope for you!

3-5: RECRUIT

You have it in you to be a bulletcatcher, but you need more training. Raise your awareness levels, assess the dangers around you and train in unarmed combat. Read *Shadow Warriors* to learn the martial arts of the ninja!

6-7: TALENT

You're on the team! Like Kasia, you're quick to catch on, tough and ready for action. You can handle both civilian and hostile environments, but you just need a little more experience to know how to handle difficult situations. Read the *Virtual Kombat* series to improve your online combat skills.

8-10: BULLETCATCHER

You are born to protect. Just like Troy, you know what to do in a dangerous situation. You always think about your VIP first and quickly assess the threat levels in any situation. If it came to it, you'd have the courage and reactions to stop a bullet for them!

Answers: 1(c), 2(d) 3(a), 4(b), 5(c), 6(d), 7(b), 8(d), 9(a), 10(c)

Do **YOU** have superpowers?

I bet you think that superpowers only exist in books and movies. But they don't ... superpowers are real!

In *S.P.E.A.R.*, each bulletcatcher has a superpower, or "talent" as it is called in the story. These talents – bulletproof, reflex, super strength, recall and blindsight – might all sound like Avenger-style superpowers, but they are powers that people *actually* possess in the real world.

Hercules Gene

Lennox has the "Hercules gene". This means his muscles are 25% larger and 50% stronger than an average human. In the real world, this condition is known as being "double-muscled" and such children do exist, like Yang Jinlong from Anhui Province in China.

Recall

Joe possesses the power of instant recall. He can remember vast amounts of information and visualise scenes he has only glimpsed for the blink of an eye. In fact, there's an incredible man called Stephen Wiltshire who can draw complete cityscapes after seeing them only for a few moments. These drawings are 100% accurate and to scale.

Blindsight

Azumi is totally blind. Yet she can see without her eyes and has the ability to glimpse into the future – a talent in the story called blindsight. There are many examples of people who have visions of the future, but even more amazing is the story of a blind boy called Ben Underwood, who could cycle, roller-skate and even play basketball, all by using echo-location like a dolphin!

Bulletproof

Troy has bulletproof skin. This sounds like a step beyond the realms of reality. But scientists have now created a skin made from goat's milk packed with spider-silk proteins that can actually stop bullets! Their idea is to replace the keratin in human skin – the protein that makes it tough – with the spider-silk proteins. This means, in the near future, there may be bulletproof kids just like Troy. Until then, you'll have to rely on bulletproof clothing!

From Magnet Men to Firemakers

There are many more amazing examples of human superpowers on the internet. There's a boy with powers like Magneto from *X-Men*, who can attract metal like a magnet; a baseball player with super-fast reflexes like Kasia; and the most incredible yet ... a man called John Chang who could set fire to objects using only his *chi* (his inner energy)!

So the next time you read *S.P.E.A.R.* or watch a superhero movie, be aware that someone in the world may possess that power ... and it could be *you*!

Go Gear

A bulletcatcher must be ready for action at all times! That's why S.P.E.A.R. supply their bulletcatchers with "Go Gear" – a kit bag full of gadgets vital for a successful mission.

The top five items in every recruit's kit bag are:

1. **Eye-cam** – a contact lens with video and photo functions. Useful to record faces in a crowd, identify a suspected threat, survey a location in advance or document the scene of an attack.

2. **First-aid kit** – the most important piece of kit. A bodyguard will use their medical skills far more than their fighting skills, and a good first-aid kit could save a person's life. Includes spray-on plasters, instant clot for gun wounds and a trauma scanner.

3. **Sunglasses** – every bulletcatcher needs these! Not only do they keep the sun out of your eyes, they have a heads-up augmented-reality display, plus a night-vision function too!

4. **Dazzler** – a small, concealable and non-lethal defence weapon. About the size of a torch, it has a laser that temporarily blinds an attacker, allowing you to escape with your VIP.

5. **Bulletproof jacket** – essential for those catchers without bulletproof talent. Made out of a liquid body armour, it's soft, flexible *and* fashionable – it will even stop a bullet fired at point-blank range. You'd be dead without it!

Quick-fire interview with *S.P.E.A.R.* author Chris Bradford

Who was your childhood hero?

Karate Kid. I really liked the way martial arts empowered him to stand up to bullies. That film kick-started my passion for martial arts.

What was your favourite book when you were younger?

The *Fighting Fantasy* series. I literally devoured them. I loved the fact that I was the hero. Perhaps that's why I became an author.

What advice would you give to your ten-year-old self?

Learn to laugh at yourself a little more. Being an emotional soul, I took everything to heart too much.

What would you be if you hadn't been a writer?

A rock star! Well, that's what I was trying to become before I came up with the *Young Samurai* idea.

If you could travel in time, where would you go first?

Sixteenth-century Japan, to meet a real samurai warrior. (I'd make sure I bowed low so I didn't get my head chopped off!)

What is the weirdest thing a fan has ever said to you?

At a book signing, I was asked by a fan, "Have you learned knife defence as a bodyguard?" I nodded and the fan held up a sharpened pencil and attacked me. Luckily my reactions were faster than his!